CHRISTMAS GAMES

EVIE ALEXANDER

EMLIN
PRESS

ISBN (eBook) 978-1-914473-20-3

ISBN (Print) 978-1-914473-21-0

ISBN (Audiobook) 978-1-914473-56-2

A CIP catalogue record for this book is available from the British Library.

www.emlinpress.com

To Elway, my miracle child

ALSO BY EVIE ALEXANDER

THE KINLOCH SERIES

Highland Games

Hollywood Games

Kissing Games

Musical Games

Wedding Games

Christmas Games

THE FOXBROOKE SERIES

One Night in Foxbrooke

Love ad Lib

An Unholy Affair

The Upper Crush

The Love Position

Christmas off Script

One Night Only

Righting Mr Wrong

Under the Influencer

Foxbrooke Extras

By Evie Alexander and Kelly Kay

EVIE & KELLY'S HOLIDAY DISASTERS SERIES

Cupid Calamity

Cookout Carnage

Christmas Chaos

Get Evie's books in all formats as well as special offers, early releases, and exclusive deals direct from her website:

www.eviealexanderbooks.com

EMLIN
PRESS

CONTENT NOTES
(INCLUDING SPOILERS)

Dear lovely reader,

First up, in case you missed this information, a version of this story was first published in the Holiday Disasters series written by me and Kelly Kay. Then, it was entitled 'No Way in a Manger', and was one of the novellas in the book Christmas Chaos. I have made some minor changes to this iteration, however it is still substantially the same work.

Secondly, all of us have different life experiences and find certain topics upsetting. Whilst it is impossible for me to know what these might be for you, I want you to be aware that this book mentions the following subjects, which may be triggering for some:

- Concerns about fertility
- A suspected miscarriage
- Hospital visits

This story is very personal to me and even though there are some crazy situations, some of the challenges Zoe faces are lifted directly from my own experiences.

However, just like in my own life, I want you to be reassured that, as ever, Christmas Games has a wonderful happy ending!

Big love,

Evie xxx

April

Rory was pretty sure he knew how babies were made, but he'd never expected it to involve holding his naked wife upside down by the ankles. He was as strong as the Highlands, but wasn't entirely confident he could hold up one hundred and forty pounds of the most precious human in his life for half an hour.

'Are you sure this is necessary?' he asked, biceps bulging as his grip tightened.

Zoe lifted her head, her long red curls swishing across the wooden floor of the cabin.

'Absolutely. It's gravity. Science.'

'I don't want to drop you.'

'You won't,' she answered cheerfully. 'And if this doesn't work, then we're going to have sex in the middle of the standing stones.'

'The ones just off the A835?'

'Yup.'

'Why?'

'Well, according to Bra—local legend, they're built over a convergence of ley lines.'

Rory gritted his teeth at the almost mention of his mother's new husband. The dowager Countess of Kinloch, and the most buttoned-up person he knew, was now married to Brad Bauer, a Hollywood superstar twelve years her junior and only seven years older than Rory himself. Brad was bonkers and Rory's mother a royal pain in the backside, but thankfully they lived in LA.

'Zoe, those stones were put up by a local farmer a few years ago for *Outlander*-obsessed tourists.'

'Really?'

'Yes.'

'Dammit. Okay, I'll ask Fiona if she knows any other good spots. There's a full moon coming up and I want to take full advantage of it.'

Rory lifted her onto the bed.

'Hey! It hasn't been half an hour yet.'

Tucking Zoe into his body, he nuzzled her cheek. 'Your face is redder than your hair, and there are definitely other things we could do to help make a baby.'

She grinned and reached down to his cock. 'Plan B?'

Rory rolled her onto her back with a growl and she giggled.

'Zoe MacGinley, as far as making babies is concerned, I'm only ever Plan A.'

A COUPLE OF HOURS LATER, RORY WAS ON THE TELEPHONE IN the Kinloch estate office, hiding behind his alter-ego of 'Greg', whilst listening to a five-minute dissertation on flowers. Posing as a member of staff usually made dealing with the public quicker and easier.

'They must be blue hydrangeas, but not those terrible electric blue ones, they have to be lavender blue as per the colour wheel I emailed. And white heather, not purple as it can't clash. To be honest with you, Greg, I can't be sure of the quality of your computer monitor, so I'm going to courier up the mood boards I've created. The actual boards. Do you appreciate the significance of this?'

Rory ran a hand into his messy blond hair and bit back a sigh. He'd heard the term 'bridezilla' before, but presumed most men getting married were happy for their only responsibility to be showing up on time.

Mr Campbell Monteith, however, was not most men. He ran a successful interior design business in Edinburgh and was marrying an American human rights lawyer and socialite he met in St. Barts. The wedding was going to be featured in magazines throughout the world, and if anything was off point, it would reflect on the creative ability of the groom.

As such, Campbell had morphed into a micromanaging groomzilla who had the estate offices on speed dial. Rory usually left dealing with people to Zoe, but she was on the other line, so he was taking one for the team.

'Yes, Mr Monteith. I fully appreciate the significance,' he replied in a thick Scottish accent.

'And I need written confirmation that the earl will be in attendance.'

Rory gazed at his wife sitting behind the desk opposite him.

'You believe the earl will be attending your wedding?' he asked loudly.

Zoe glanced up with a guilty expression, before swivelling her chair to face the wall and continuing her own conversation.

'Yes, Greg. Do you even read your emails?' asked Campbell.

'I appreciate Lord MacGinley is a busy man, but I'd like to speak to him at least once in the next six months.'

And this is why I put on a Scottish accent and call myself Greg, Rory thought, circling the astronomical figure Zoe had scrawled on a piece of paper the last time he'd suggested they cancel this particular booking.

'I'm sure that can be arranged, Mr Monteith.'

'Good. Make it so, Greg. Make it so.'

Rory finished the conversation with as much politeness as he could muster, then stalked across the room to his wife's desk.

Time for payback.

Zoe's chair was facing away with her long legs extended and her feet propped up on a two-drawer filing cabinet.

Rory sat on the edge of the desk behind her and put his hands on her shoulders, massaging away the tension created from a half-hour conversation with a new supplier.

Zoe leaned back into his touch, her 'hmms' of affirmation directed down the phone morphing into sounds of enjoyment directed at him. Rory knew her body intimately, and every little shudder and noise of pleasure made his cock twitch. Zoe's wild curls were perched on the top of her head, secured in place with a pencil, leaving her neck exposed. He trailed soft kisses from her hairline down to her ear and she shuddered.

Smiling, he gently bit the lobe.

'Ahhh! Er! Oh no, um, I thought I saw a mouse. What? No! We don't have any mice in the castle,' she babbled.

Rory ran a hand inside her top, rubbing a hardened nipple through her bra.

'Oh god! Um, it's a spider. I'm so sorry, I have arachnophobia. Can I ring you back in five minutes?'

'Fifteen,' Rory murmured.

'Sorry, I meant five times three.'

He reached inside her bra.

'Fift... Agh! Call you right back!' she cried, ending the call.

Turning her chair, Rory lifted Zoe onto his lap. She wrapped herself around him, her tongue meeting his as she squirmed against his hardness. He wanted to tease her, to torment her for agreeing he would attend some random person's wedding. But he didn't care anymore. It would be a minor inconvenience in a life now filled with love and happiness, all thanks to his crazy, brilliant, firecracker of a wife.

The phone rang.

It was always ringing.

Zoe pulled away with a whimper. 'I should answer it.'

Rory ripped the cable from the wall.

'Rory!'

He shrugged and grinned, tugging her T-shirt out of her jeans. 'I'll fix it later.'

'And I forgot I've got a meeting at the bakery with Margaret in ten minutes.'

'I'll get you off in five,' he growled, pulling her top and bra off.

THAT AFTERNOON, IN A BREAK BETWEEN CALLS, ZOE HAD scheduled a meeting to discuss the 'C' word...

Before he met his wife, Rory considered Christmas to be the one day a year he went through the motions if he was with his army unit, or gritted his teeth if he was with his mother. However, as the Earl of Kinloch, pimping out his castle to pay the bills, it appeared he needed to be thinking about Christmas the previous Boxing Day.

It didn't help that his wife was a believer. No matter what was associated with the holidays, Zoe believed in it all. Santa, the Nativity, mistletoe, stockings, mulled wine, mince pies, carols and Slade. Everything was up for grabs. She might be humming 'Oh Little Town of Bethlehem' one minute, then 'Merry Christmas Everybody' the next. If this level of commitment to what Rory considered a manufactured holiday to celebrate capitalism was exhibited by one of his friends, he would have thought they were deranged. With Zoe, however, he was grudgingly forced to admit it was endearing.

But if his wife loved Christmas, stationery came a close second. These two obsessions had come together and were currently making sweet, sweet love across one entire wall of the estate office. An A3 calendar from Rymans was too insubstantial for what Zoe needed, so she'd created her own with washi tape, Post-its, Sharpies and stickers. Each time a task included her, she stuck a sticker of an angel next to it.

When Rory was needed, she stuck up one of The Grinch.

'So, in order that you can't claim I don't run things by you,' she began.

He raised an eyebrow.

'Which of course is nonsense,' she ploughed on, staring at a point an inch above his head.

Rory cleared his throat.

'So, I—' she continued.

'The Monteith–Kowalski wedding?' he interrupted.

She grinned. 'Did you see how much they're paying? The profits should cover a staff wage for a year.'

'Yes, I saw. I'm surprised to wake each morning and find you haven't tattooed it on the back of my hand overnight.'

Zoe's expression was far too excited at that prospect for comfort, so Rory fixed her with one of his stern looks.

She responded the way she always did, by laughing.

He shook his head with a resigned smile. 'Okay, get on with it. I need to check on the cows at Alasdair's farm.'

'Right! Okay! So, from May, every other weekend is booked

up with weddings, and the rest of the time the castle is open for tourists. It's great, but you know it only just covers wages and we're not yet fully in profit.'

Rory nodded. The busier they became, the more staff were needed. But wages were the biggest drain on their coffers, so the two of them were working seven days a week trying to get everything done and keep costs down.

'This year I want to go all in. We've got the ceilidh, which is free for the village, but I want to have another one for the public and charge for entry.'

That made sense, but Rory knew his wife was softening him up for a killer blow.

'And we're going to hire out the entire castle to a private party for Christmas week.'

'What private party? Who are they?'

'They're friends of, erm, "He Who Shall Not Be Named".'

'Please tell me he's not going to be there too?'

'No! No, I promise. He's shooting *Fight Dragon Club*. Your mum assured me they would be staying in LA the whole time.'

Thank god for that. When Rory had visited his mother and her new husband, he found their lifestyle to be even more irritating and vacuous than he could ever have imagined.

'I want to do a light installation in the castle gardens starting October half-term and running into December,' Zoe continued. 'With wreath-making workshops, mulled wine, carollers et cetera.'

Rory nodded. It would be an insane amount of work, but these were great ideas. However, his wife had a look he knew all too well, and it made the back of his neck tingle.

'What part of "et cetera" involves me?'

'Erm, you need to grow a beard.'

'Why?' he asked, already fearing the answer.

'I want you to play Santa.'

'Zoe, I'm thirty-five, not sixty-five. Go into The King's Arms and choose someone else. Every night is like a Father Christmas convention there.'

'But they're not the Earl of Kinloch,' she protested.

'Do you think some snot-nosed little kid is going to care?'

Her cheeks were getting redder. This was not a good sign.

'Zoe?'

'We shouldn't be ageist. We need an equal opportunity Santa.'

Rory closed his eyes and saw exactly what Zoe had in mind.

'So, you're going to advertise a day when all the world and his wife can come and sit on my knee and say what they want me to put in their stocking?'

His eyes opened at his wife's howls of laughter.

'Oh my god, Rory, that's genius! "Tell the Earl of Kinloch how you'd like your stocking stuffed". This is amazing! We should do a week of it!'

'One day. And only humans in single digits.'

'What about the oldies? Under ten and over seventy?'

'Are you joking? The pensioners are the bloody worst! Since I carried Mrs McCreedie out of her house last year after the lorry crashed into it, she's been more than a little handsy.'

Zoe was now crying with laughter. 'Okay, nine and under, I promise.'

'And do I really need to grow a beard for one day?'

'You need to fully embrace the spirit of Christmas,' she said, wiping her eyes. 'And besides, maybe if we're lucky you can play Joseph to my Mary?'

Rory drew her into his arms. 'If that's what you want.'

'I always wanted to play Mary in the nativity at school,' she murmured into his chest. 'But I was always a sheep. Or a giraffe.'

'A giraffe?'

'Because I was tall. At least I never had to play the octopus.'

Huh?

'Vital part of every modern-day nativity. You've gotta move with the times.'

'Humph.'

They stood in silence.

'What if it doesn't happen?' Zoe asked, quietly. 'What if we can't have a baby?'

Rory held her a little tighter. 'It will. We just need to give it a bit more time.'

She looked at him. 'Do you think we should book in for some tests?'

Her expression broke his heart, so he forced a smile. 'Whatever you want. I'm here for you.'

✤ 2 ✤

Two days later, Zoe took a break from admin and strolled through Kinloch to a modern housing estate on the edge of the village, where her friend Fiona lived with her family.

As a child, Zoe had spent a summer in Kinloch where she'd met Fiona for the first time. They were the same age and shared the same sense of humour. Now, two decades on, Zoe was back for good and Fiona had become one of her closest friends.

As the front door opened, an auburn-haired toddler barrelled out, his arms outstretched.

'Dohee! Dohee!'

Zoe lifted him. 'Hey Liam, you gorgeous little monkey. How goes it?'

A plastic car was thrust in her face. 'Brrrrrrrrmmm! Brrrrrrrrmmm!' he replied, splattering her face with saliva.

Fiona grabbed her son. 'No brum brum in people's faces, mister, or Dohee won't ever come back.' She pulled a face at Zoe. 'Sorry about that. Try and think of it as strengthening your immune system. Come on through and I'll put the kettle on.'

Inside, Zoe sat at the kitchen table with Liam next to her in his high chair as her friend bustled about. She tried to keep her eyes on Fiona's face, but her gaze kept falling to her rounded belly. Would she ever get pregnant?

Zoe had always wanted to be a mother, and now she'd met Rory, it was all she seemed to think about. Well, that and jumping him at every opportunity. She kept expecting their first flush of passion to fade, but it only seemed to be getting stronger. If the amount of sex correlated with the ability to get pregnant, she should have been carrying octuplets well over a year ago.

'Milk?' Fiona asked, startling her from her daydreams.

'Yeah, thanks. Ooh! And you've got choccy bickies, too.'

'Bickie! Bickie!'

Fiona broke a biscuit in half and handed one side to Liam, who stuffed it in his mouth sideways.

'Jesus wept, love, not like that!' Fiona retrieved it and broke it in half again. 'Honestly, Zo, he loves these. I left the room to pee yesterday and came back to find he'd dragged a chair to the counter and was trying to climb up to get to the cupboard. Sneaky little bugger.'

'Bugga! Bugga! Bugga!' yelled Liam excitedly.

'Fuck's sake! I keep forgetting he can talk.'

'Ucks ay! Ucks ay, Mummy!'

Zoe snorted with laughter, which set Liam off even more. Fiona attempted to be stern with her son, but he seemed to know from her expression that this word would get the maximum reaction from the most important person in his life.

'Just wait till your father gets home, Mister,' said Fiona, wagging her finger at her son.

Fiona's husband, Duncan, worked as an electrician and rope

access specialist on oil rigs in the North Sea and was away two weeks out of every four.

'How's it going?' Zoe asked.

Fiona's hand went to her bump. Zoe knew how anxious she was each time her husband left. Her mum, Morag, had been pregnant with Fiona's younger brother, Jamie, when her father had died on the rigs doing the exact same job that her husband now did. Fiona usually tried to hide her concern, but now the smiles about Liam's antics slipped away.

'Not great, to be honest, Zo.' She rubbed at a spot on the table. 'With the state of the world, half the crew doesn't know if they'll be laid off tomorrow, then reinstated the week later. Dunc's fed up with the uncertainty.'

Zoe gave her friend's hand a squeeze.

'You must be sick of me moaning by now,' Fiona grimaced.

'No! Of course not. Complain all you like. That's what friends are for.'

'It's like we've made a pact with the devil. The money's so good we can afford to buy our forever home. But I don't know how I'm going to cope once the new baby comes.'

'Babyyyyy,' repeated Liam, solemnly.

Zoe understood. One child looked hard enough, but having to be a single mum half the time with a newborn as well didn't sound like much fun.

'You know you can always ask me to help?'

'Zo, you're so busy, it's a miracle I see you at all.'

Zoe sighed. Fiona was right. She'd come to Scotland looking for a quieter life but had ended up the Countess of Kinloch, married to Thor's overly libidinous brother, and fifty per cent responsible for a castle and thousands of acres of land. Something was going to have to give.

She took a gulp of tea. 'Fi, is the milk off?'

'Fresh this morning.' Fiona sipped hers. 'Tastes okay to me.'

Zoe took another mouthful. 'It tastes weird.'

'Decaf teabags?'

'Nah, I've been drinking decaf here for the last six months.'

'Zoeeeeeeee...' Fiona drew out the last syllable, her eyes sparkling.

Zoe shook her head. 'I can't be. I tested negative again this morning.'

'Are you late?'

'Four days, but that's normal. You know my cycles are all over the place.'

Fiona leaned back in her chair and pulled a pregnancy test from a low drawer, placing it on the table.

'You could do another one?'

Zoe shrugged. 'It'll still be negative. They always are.'

'Well then, you'd know?'

'I don't know, Fi.'

'Zoe, Zoe, Zoe, Zoe,' Fiona chanted, getting louder and louder.

'Dohee! Dohee! Dohee!' yelled Liam.

'Alright, alright!' She laughed. 'I'll go pee on a stick.'

A minute later, Zoe was back and laid the test face down on a wad of toilet paper. Fiona set the timer on the oven, and they waited. Even Liam was silent, his eyes flicking between them as he tried to figure out what was going on.

The beep of the oven went through Zoe with a crack of adrenaline. Every time was the same. The nervous hope, the flash-forwards to possible futures, then the deflating disappointment at the sight of only one blue line.

'Go on then, look,' Fiona urged.

Zoe flipped it over as if she wasn't bothered and stared at two blue lines. She blinked. Was it true? Was she really pregnant? She looked in astonishment at Fiona's shocked face.

'Well, bugger me, Zo,' Fiona exhaled. 'You're going to have a baby.'

'Bugga mee! Bugga mee! Babyyyyyyy!' agreed Liam.

⁘

RORY'S FOREHEAD WAS DAMP WITH SWEAT, HIS HEART racing.

'Come on, Zoe, push, lass!' Alasdair yelled.

The sounds of her pain echoed around them. Things were not going well.

'Rory, talk to her. I'm going in again.'

Rory stroked Zoe's long red curls from her eyes. They were wide and panicked, her breath hot and fast against his face.

'It's okay,' he said. 'Listen to my voice. It's okay.'

Zoe bellowed with pain, the sound nearly knocking him off his feet.

'I've got a foot!' called Alasdair. 'Get the rope! Quick!'

Rory grabbed it and looped it around the protruding leg. It was wet and smeared with blood. Zoe cried out again, and his heart lurched.

'Now pull!'

Rory pulled and Alasdair's gloved arm disappeared back into Zoe, emerging with another leg.

'We've got him! Come on, Rory!'

They heaved, and the baby slithered out onto the floor. It had curly red hair, just like its mother. Alasdair cleaned its face, and they rubbed the body until it took a few breaths. Rory felt like he'd been holding his for hours.

'Well done,' said Alasdair, patting him on the back. 'I don't think that would have ended well for either of them if you hadn't been here.'

Zoe was now licking her baby, looking far less traumatised than Rory felt. He stared at his bloodied hands.

'Alasdair,' he began, his voice scratchy and low.

'Yes, lad?'

'Why did you have to call her Zoe?'

Alasdair's brow furrowed as if Rory had just asked him to explain why the sun rose every morning.

'Her hair, of course. Never seen a hairy coo with curlier. Do you want to name the calf? He's going to be a strapping wee fella, I just know.'

Rory shook his head. He'd been in life-or-death situations more times than he could remember, but nothing ever quite like this.

There was the sound of a vehicle pulling up in the yard outside.

'Finally!' said Alasdair. 'That should be the vet.' He pushed to his feet. 'Oh, I've got the perfect name – I bet he makes the cover of *The Highland Times*.'

Rory's heart sank at Alasdair's excited face.

'I'm going to call him Brad!'

DRIVING BACK TOWARDS KINLOCH AND A RELIABLE PHONE connection, Rory's phone buzzed repeatedly with notifications. Was something wrong? He glanced at the screen. Most of the messages were from Zoe, asking after her cow and wanting to know when Rory was coming back.

Pulling into the back courtyard of the castle, he cut the engine. This was the first birth he'd attended that had been touch and go. Was that what human birth was like? Was this what Zoe was going to have to experience if they ever got pregnant?

He ran his hands into his hair, tugging at the roots. He

wanted to talk it out, but didn't want to share these fears with Zoe and freak her out. Would his best mate, Charlie, understand? Probably not.

Getting out of the truck, Rory went into the castle. He could deal with his problems on his own.

INSIDE THE ESTATE OFFICE, ZOE ENDED HER CALL ABRUPTLY when Rory entered.

'Roryyyyyyyy!' She ran to his side and threw her arms around his neck. 'I love you, I love you, I love you, I LOVE YOU!'

He grinned, his heart lifting. They didn't need a baby, they just needed each other.

'I love you, too. Sorry I'm late. Zoe had her calf.'

'Eek! Boy or girl?'

'Boy.'

'Called?'

He pulled a face, and she laughed. 'Oh, my god. Did Alasdair name him after you?'

Rory shook his head. 'Think of the worst possible name he could have chosen.'

Zoe affected a look of concentration, but he knew she'd guessed the name by the sparkle in her eyes.

'Arnold? After my dad?'

He shook his head again.

'Stuart? After yours?'

'No.'

'Um, was the calf named after your step-fa—'

He growled in warning.

She shrieked with laughter. 'I bet Alasdair thinks it'll get him on the cover of *The Times* or Brad's Instagram feed. God, people are nuts. You know the last three boys born in Kinloch were all called Bradley?'

He nodded.

'They should have been christened Rory,' she continued. 'That's a far better name.'

She kissed him and all his cares melted away.

'Your stubble feels funny.'

'I can shave it off.'

'December twenty-sixth. You can be like a sheep and have an annual shearing.'

Rory rolled his eyes as he grinned at her. Zoe was a lunatic, but she was *his* lunatic.

Pulling away, she went to her desk. 'Close your eyes. And hold out your hands.'

'Have I forgotten my birthday again?'

'Nope. Stay still.'

Something light was placed in his palm.

'Okay, you can open them now.'

He did, looking first at Zoe's face, then at the white stick in his hand.

'I'm pregnant!' she screamed. 'We're having a baby!'

❧ 3 ❧

Breathe in, two, three, four, and hold, two, three, four. Breathe out, two, three, four…

Rory's jaw clenched tight as he did the breathing exercise Zoe's best friend, Sam, shared with him, saying it calmed her down when she was stressed. Right now, with Zoe curled up on his lap on the phone to her mother, Rory needed all the help he could get to hide his emotions. He was absolutely terrified.

'I don't feel pregnant. Should I feel pregnant? What am I meant to be feeling? Oh my god, Mum, I'm pregnant!'

Zoe's mother, Mary, was on speakerphone and her laugh was warm.

'My darling girl, you might not feel anything for weeks, but you could get very tired and nauseous. You need to rest.'

'But I don't want to! I've got to get everything organised for Christmas.'

Oh god. Fucking Christmas. Rory's heart rate spiked as he tried to work out when Zoe might give birth. *December? January?*

'Zoe, love, it's the beginning of April,' said her mother.

'Yes, but I'm due mid-January, so what if the baby comes early? I can't leave anything to chance. Or to The Grinch.'

'Rory, are you listening to this slander?'

He let his breath go. He had to keep it together.

'Yes, Mary,' he replied. 'Although if you weren't on the other end of the phone, I would have already tuned out.'

'Oi!' said Zoe, wiggling the fingers of her free hand. 'I know how ticklish you are. These digits are deadly weapons and I'm not afraid to use them.'

Rory flinched. The thought of being tickled was almost enough to displace the fear that his wife was finally pregnant.

'Apologies, Mary. What I meant to say is that I am tuned one hundred per cent to Radio Zoe and am hanging on her every word.'

'Oh dear.' Her mother laughed. 'That's your first mistake. If I paid attention to half of what Arnold said, I'd go mad or fall asleep.'

'Mum! This is serious! Christmas is serious! I've got to be prepared.'

Breathe in, two, three, four, and hold, two, three, four. Breathe out, two, three, four, and hold, two, three, four. Rory's brain stumbled forward through the year. Sod Christmas preparations. What about preparing the cabin for the baby?

In the army, he'd been trained to assess every environment for risks, and right now, thinking about splinters from the floor, burns from the Rayburn, slips in the bathroom and falls from the furniture, the cabin was looking more dangerous than a temple trap from an *Indiana Jones* movie.

'Darling,' Mary continued. 'I had to be induced with you at forty-two weeks, and most first-time mums give birth ten days after they're supposed to. You'll be fine. This is going to be your last quiet Christmas for quite a while, so you need to enjoy it.'

Breathe in, two, three, four, and hold, two, three, four. Breathe out...

'When does Dad get home? Does he have his mobile on him? I want you to tell him the moment he gets in.'

'He left it at home again. He'll be back about seven, just as I'm heading out to choir practice. Will you still be at the castle?'

'No, we'll be home by then. Tell him to take his phone tomorrow and I'll ring him in the morning.'

'Okay, love, will do. Now rest up and let your wonderful husband take care of you.'

Yes. This was something Rory knew he could do. As Zoe said goodbye to her mother, she shifted in his lap.

'Rory...'

'Hmmm?'

'I think I need to lie down.'

Panic flared. 'Are you okay?'

She giggled at his response and guided his hands under her top to her breasts. 'I need you to take care of me.'

Relief flooded through him. They were back on solid ground. He brushed his lips against her throat and she shivered.

'Well, we'd better get you home then,' he murmured.

THERE WAS NOTHING MORE INTOXICATING TO RORY THAN getting his wife off. Over and over again. His own orgasms were always spectacular and carried a risk of aneurysm, but the sensation was deeper and more complex with Zoe. The taste of her on his tongue, the feel of her fevered skin, the way her thighs clamped around his head, the sound of her screaming his name. It was a rush like no other. And now, making her come was the ultimate distraction from the baby elephant in his mental room.

However, if making her come was the source of his greatest pleasure, being interrupted whilst doing so was the source of his greatest *dis*pleasure.

Bang! Bang! Bang!

'Rory,' she gasped. 'There's someone at the—'

He flicked his tongue faster. Zoe's thighs were trembling. She was so close. Unless the cabin was on fire, he wasn't going to stop.

'Hang on!' Zoe cried to whoever was outside. 'I'm commmm-mmmmmmmminnnngggggggg!'

Her body stiffened, and he held her tightly, licking harder, pushing the wave of her orgasm faster through her till her body convulsed on the bed.

'Oh my god, oh my god, oh my god,' she gasped.

When Zoe's body went limp, Rory gently pulled away and covered her with the duvet. He was still dressed, so adjusted his cock for decency, stalked to the door and opened it a crack.

'Fiona, is everything okay?'

'It is now. Ish,' she replied. 'Congratulations, by the way. Is your mum pleased?'

'She doesn't know. We've only told Zoe's parents so far.'

'Well, they must have accidentally let the cat out of the bag, or the bun out of the oven.' She passed him her phone. 'Don't panic, it's gone now. This is just a screenshot.'

Rory stared at Brad's face on his Instagram feed. He looked deranged with excitement. The caption across the bottom screamed: 'I'm gonna be a Pop Pop!!!'

What. The. Fuck.

'Luckily, Sam saw it pretty much the moment it was posted and called me. I told her Zoe was about ten seconds pregnant and hadn't told anyone yet. So Sam phoned Brad and made him take it down. We think it was only up for about ten minutes.'

'What's going on?' Zoe asked from behind him.

Rory handed her the phone. 'It's been deleted now.'

'Oh god.' Her hand went to her stomach. 'But only Mum knows! And I told her not to tell anyone.'

'Your dad must have accidentally said something.'

Her eyes welled up. 'I wanted this to be a secret. Something just for us. Even if only for a little while.'

He pulled her into his arms. 'I know.'

'And the first three months are the most...' She broke off as if she couldn't say what they were all thinking.

Rory turned to Fiona. 'You okay to stay with Zoe for twenty minutes while I drive up the hill and attempt to murder my mother's husband with only the power of my voice?'

Fiona grinned. 'Yep, no worries.'

'Will you phone my dad too?' Zoe asked. 'If it was him, he's going to be devastated.'

He kissed the top of her head. 'Of course. He hasn't done anything wrong.'

Zoe frowned. 'Be nice to Brad. He's just excited, that's all. He doesn't mean any harm.'

Rory's response was a harrumph. He wasn't going to make any promises he couldn't keep.

RORY PULLED INTO A LAYBY WHERE HE KNEW THERE WAS reception. He was perfectly happy insulated from the rest of the world with Zoe at the cabin, but if something happened to her or the baby, the lack of phone signal wasn't practical. He rubbed his stubble and sighed. Things were going to change whether he wanted them to or not.

Taking a deep breath, he rang his mother's number in LA.

'Why didn't you tell me?' she demanded the moment the call connected.

'*That's* what you're leading with?'

'Is that Rory?' Brad said in the background. 'Can I speak to him? I need to—'

'Bradley!' his mother barked.

'Yes, Countess,' he replied instantly. The sound was muffled as if Barbara was holding the phone to her chest, but Brad's obedient tone reminded Rory of his army days.

'Go to the room.'

Huh?

'Yes, Countess.'

What the actual...?

Rory heard his mother's heels clicking across the floor, then the sound of a door closing.

She sighed. 'Rory, I want to apologise on behalf of my husband. I was out and Bradley rang Arnold to chat about fishing. Arnold thought we knew, and Bradley became overly excited about becoming a...' she cleared her throat, '...about your pregnancy, and wanted to share that excitement with the world.'

Rory paused and gazed out of the truck window. Apologies were so rare from his mother he half expected to see a sounder of pigs soaring across the glen.

'I wish you'd told me first,' she continued. 'So I could have handled him appropriately.'

'Mum. We only found out this afternoon.'

'Well, we're very happy for you, dear, and looking forward to helping you run this pregnancy properly.'

'What?' Growing up, Rory remembered his mother being about as maternal as a cuckoo. Was she about to morph into Mary Poppins?

'What is there to run?' he asked. 'Zoe's growing a baby.'

His mother laughed. 'My dear boy. Any fool can have a baby. Your wife is gestating the future Earl of Kinloch.'

Rory pinched the bridge of his nose. Once again, he wished he was just a simple carpenter.

'Mother. There's a fifty per cent chance it will be a girl.'

Barbara sniffed. 'And, of course, that scenario would be delightful. Every child is a blessing.'

He rolled his eyes.

'So,' she continued, 'we'll have a press release drafted for you in the next few hours, and I'll start compiling lists of the best doctors and researching the correct name. Tell Zoe not to worry about a thing. She needs to rest. I can take care of it all.'

'Mum—'

'You must give her my fondest regards. I know I may not sound it, Rory, but I'm extremely excited. Not in the same way as Bradley, of course. I'm not American. However, I'm thrilled for you all the same and looking forward to being a grandmother—'

'Mum—'

'Good grief! That makes me sound old. Thank goodness Honey Boo-Boo is arriving in an hour for my personal training session. She may have an absolutely ridiculous name, but she nearly beat Bradley at arm wrestling. An extraordinary woman.'

'Mum! You need to back off and give Zoe some space. One in four pregnancies doesn't even make it past three months.'

There was a pause.

'That's true, although he's half MacGinley, so stronger than the common herd.'

'Jesus Christ! Zoe's stronger than I am and you know it.'

Barbara sighed. 'Well, she'd better be. Birthing you was a challenge and now look at the size of you. Unless you elect for a caesarean section, your wife will be attempting to deliver an ox.'

$$\maltese \quad 4 \quad \maltese$$

May. Six weeks + two

For the two weeks since finding out his wife was pregnant, Rory kept his operating system set to non-baby status. Zoe didn't look pregnant and told him she didn't feel any different. Therefore, she wasn't really going to give birth in eight months, and his life could continue contentedly on.

That was until they were driving down the side of the glen towards the cabin and Zoe stiffened.

'Stop the truck!'

Rory screeched to a halt at the side of the road, and Zoe threw herself out, bending over and breathing heavily. By the time he reached her, Bandit was already at her side, rubbing against her leg.

Rory tentatively stroked Zoe's back. 'Are you okay? Do you think you're going to be sick?'

Hands braced on her thighs, she was breathing slowly in

through her nose and out through her mouth. Anxiety squeezed his chest.

'I don't think so. It just came on so quickly.'

She's alright. Get it together. 'How do you feel now?'

She cranked herself vertical, and he examined her face.

Giggling, she ran her fingers over his frown lines. 'I'm fine. I'm sure it's just a one-off. You took that last bend too fast and left my tummy behind. I think *I* should drive the rest of the way.'

The relief was so palpable Rory thought he might float away. *She's okay. Everything's okay.*

He raised an eyebrow. 'You think you're a safer driver than me?'

'I never said I was *safer*. Being driven by me is more exciting. Therefore, I'm a *better* driver than you.'

God, how he loved her. Rory tried to keep his face stern, but could feel the corners of his mouth twitching.

'I prefer the term "terrifying",' he replied. 'When you're at the wheel, it's like playing chicken with death.'

Zoe grinned. 'And doesn't it make you feel alive? You're living in the moment. It's like mindfulness training. Very Buddhist. I'm basically a spiritual guru.'

Rory leaned down, his lips almost touching hers. 'Well,' he murmured, 'I do like worshipping you.'

Her breath hitched. 'Do you, er, fancy entering my temple?'

He tugged her closer. 'Yes, I do. Many, many times.'

RORY HAD HOPED THE NAUSEA WAS A ONE-OFF, BUT OVER THE next twenty-four hours he knew it was here to stay.

'I thought it was meant to be morning sickness, not all-the-time sickness,' Zoe grumbled as she lay on the sofa, Basil, her pet Dumbo rat, sniffing her hand and Bandit at her feet on the floor.

The animals seemed to know instinctively that something was different and wanted to stay close to Zoe at all times. Bandit, in particular, was being extra protective, and Rory had to put him outside whenever they had sex, in case the dog thought Zoe was in pain. The last thing he wanted was his bollocks bitten off.

'You always like to buck the trend,' he replied as he fed the Rayburn more wood. 'Are you sure I can't persuade you to eat something?'

She pulled a face. 'The thought of food makes me feel sick. The only thing I like the look of right now is you, but that's not going to sustain me for the next seven and a half months.'

'Oh, I don't know. Apparently—'

She threw a sofa cushion at him. 'Don't even go there, Rory MacGinley.'

Opening a cupboard, he retrieved a tube of Pringles. His diet may have consisted of water, salt and beef from the estate herd, but Zoe was now living off crisps, smoked salmon and pickled gherkins.

She perked up. 'Ooh! Prawn cocktail flavour.'

Ten minutes later, the tube was empty.

'Thank you for not saying anything,' she said as Basil scouted for crumbs.

'Well, apparently once you pop, you can't stop,' he replied. 'I'm just glad to see you eating.'

She yawned. 'I'm so tired, Rory, and there's too much to do.'

He didn't know how to reply. Zoe was right. He had no idea how they were going to get everything done for Christmas on top of their already insane workload.

'I can make it work,' he told her with as much conviction as he could muster. 'Greg will just have to put in extra hours at the office, that's all.'

'But all my plans. They need sorting *now*.'

He rubbed his chin. 'Well, the beard is in hand. That's one thing you don't need to worry about.'

'Your beard isn't going to sell Christmas, no matter *how* impressive it is.'

'I think it's at least worthy of one of your crazy calendar ideas.'

As soon as the words were out of his mouth, Zoe's face lit up and Rory's heart sank.

'Oh my god, YES! You can do a sexy Santa calendar!'

His head shook so fast, her face was a blur. 'No, no, no, no, no, no fucking way.'

She slumped back onto the sofa. 'Okay,' she grumbled. 'No calendar.'

Rory knelt on the floor and took her hand. 'Whatever Santa fantasies you have inside your beautifully bonkers head, I promise I will do my best to indulge them. Do you want to cross anything off your wish list tonight?'

She smiled. 'Can I see your north pole?'

He raised an eyebrow. 'Only if I get to lick your baubles.'

June. Nine weeks

RORY WAS AN ONION OF ANXIETY. AT HIS CORE WAS THE deep-rooted belief that he would be a terrible father. He could unpick the thought with logic and common sense, but the unconscious fear still remained that he would, through DNA or imprinting, behave the same way his father had towards him.

Built over this were layers upon layers of stress. Would Zoe be okay? Would she survive labour and birth? Was the baby healthy? How could he take some of her workload away? Even if he managed to rationalise one worry, there was always another one hiding underneath.

He wanted to talk to his best friend about it all, but Charlie was in LA and their time zones never seemed to match. Rory was also working around the clock to try and keep on top of the everyday running of the estate, all the weddings they had booked, and the planning for Christmas.

But for all the weight on his shoulders, Rory knew he had it easy compared to Zoe. The only time she wasn't exhausted or nauseous was when she was asleep, the brief moments she could eat, or when she was orgasming. Keeping her satisfied was a duty he undertook with absolute dedication.

Right now, she was riding him, and he was trying to keep his own climax at bay until she'd had her third. Her expression had been one of bliss, but her closed eyes were twitching in a way that worried him.

He squeezed her thighs. 'You okay?'

Her eyes snapped open. 'Yes, I'm fine.' She moved faster, but was now biting her lower lip.

'Zoe, stop! Are you *sure* you're alright?'

Getting off him, she sat on the bed cross-legged, holding her stomach.

Rory got to his knees, his heart pounding.

'I don't know,' she said. 'My tummy hurts, that's all.'

'What can I do? Hot water bottle? Cup of tea? Should I go up the hill and ring the midwife?'

Zoe's face was pale. 'No, I'm fine. It's nothing.'

'Are you—'

'No, no, no, no, no!'

Fuck! 'What's wrong?'

Leaping off the bed, she ran for the bathroom, leaving a puddle of blood behind on the sheet.

It was huge.

Fear strangled him, turning his vision white. Stumbling off the bed, he followed her, blood roaring in his head. He had to hold it together even though he was being torn apart.

Zoe was sitting on the toilet, rocking back and forth, her hands clasped in her lap.

Rory knelt by her side. 'What can I do? Shall we go to the hospital?'

She was shivering. 'Can you clean the bed?' she whispered. 'I don't want to see it.'

He nodded and dashed out. He had to deal with Zoe's shock first, so returned to drape a blanket over her shoulders and help her feet into fluffy slippers. She murmured something, and he crouched down.

'What did you say, love?'

'It's common to bleed during pregnancy. I'm sure everything's fine.'

'I know it is,' he replied, not believing a word he was saying. 'Can I get you anything else before I deal with the sheets?'

She shook her head.

Closing the bathroom door behind him, Rory stared at the bed. There was bleeding during pregnancy, then there was this. He'd seen blood before, and he'd seen death. But nothing had ever felt like this. His heart was being ripped to shreds.

He had done this.

He had hurt the love of his life, and most likely cost her the thing she wanted more than anything else in the world.

Clenching his jaw against the rising tide of nausea, he pulled the sheet off the bed. The blood had soaked through to the woollen mattress protector. He dragged it off. The stain continued, as if burrowing its way to the centre of his soul.

How could he ever forgive himself?

Chucking the linen in a bucket of cold water, Rory scrubbed the mattress as best he could, then rushed back to check on Zoe.

'How are you doing?'

She shrugged. Her cheeks were dry, and somehow that made everything even worse.

'I don't want to leave you, but I should call the midwife, see what they say?'

She nodded. 'Yes, please.'

'I'll be as quick as I can.'

Pulling some pads from the cabinet, he put them on the side. 'I'll just grab you some water and some painkillers.'

The nod of her head was almost imperceptible.

Returning with a glass, a packet of paracetamol, and a sleepy Basil, he placed Zoe's pet in her hands.

'I know he's not as handsome as me, but he's probably better at looking after you.'

Zoe tried to smile, but her lower lip was wobbling.

Rory wanted to stay, but knew he needed to speak to a professional.

'I love you, Zoe. It's going to be okay. I promise.'

He kissed the top of her head, then left.

Nine weeks + one

ZOE PASSED MORE BLOOD OVERNIGHT. RORY HELD HER WHEN she managed to nod off, then changed her pad when she woke up. She didn't want to look at it, and he understood. Until they knew for sure what had happened, he wanted her to believe it was all okay.

Despite how much he rationalised it, he couldn't believe there was still a baby there. The midwife had made an appointment for them at EPAU, the Early Pregnancy Assessment Unit, so they set off early that morning for Raigmore hospital.

'I don't feel sick anymore,' Zoe said quietly after they'd been driving for a few minutes.

Rory's hands gripped the steering wheel tighter as he tried to keep his voice calm. 'That could just be adrenaline?'

'I don't know. I just keep waiting to feel like I did yesterday, but I don't.'

'Let's see what they say, eh?'

Tears ran silently down Zoe's cheeks. 'I think it's clear what they're going to say.'

Rory reached over to clasp her hand in his. He had no idea how to make this right, but he was going to die trying.

The waiting room was filled with miserable-looking couples who avoided eye contact. Rory gave their details to the receptionist, then they waited, Zoe sitting on his lap, her tears wetting the front of his shirt.

'Mrs MacGinley?'

This was it. Schrodinger's baby. Their child was there and not there. Both realities existed until confirmed either way. Taking her hand, they entered the consulting room.

Inside, Zoe told the nurse and sonographer what had happened.

'Do you know if you passed the embryo?' the nurse asked.

Zoe shook her head. 'Not yet.'

'Okay, we're going to do a transvaginal ultrasound and see what's going on, okay?'

She nodded.

'If you can take your bottoms off, we can take a look.'

The sonographer applied a strip of lube to what looked like a dildo.

What the fuck? Rory cleared his throat. 'Erm, is that, er, safe?'

The woman smiled knowingly. 'That's what *all* the husbands ask. It may be bigger than what you're used to seeing, but I assure you it's perfectly safe. And it's only going in a couple of inches.'

Breathe in, two, three, four, and hold, two, three, four...

Rory clasped Zoe's hand as she lay back. This was the moment they confirmed what he already knew.

'Okay, let's take a wee look, shall we?'

His heart was thudding inside his chest. Tears ran down the sides of Zoe's face and he gently wiped them away, feeling them as his own.

'So, if you look at the screen, you can see your baby there.'

'I know,' said Zoe. 'I haven't passed it yet.'

'And there's the heartbeat.'

Rory's grip on her hand tightened. 'What?'

'Your baby's heartbeat. They're doing fine and dandy.'

Zoe sobbed, and he hugged her into his chest. 'It's okay, Zoe. Our baby's okay.'

Our baby. Our baby. Our baby. The words bounced around inside his head. There was a future child inside her, and he'd nearly killed it.

The woman removed the probe and handed Zoe a wad of paper towels.

'You can put your clothes back on now.'

Zoe was still crying so much that her body was clumsy, so Rory helped her dress, then sat her on his lap and curled his arms protectively around her.

'Why did this happen?' he asked the sonographer, needing to hear from them if it was his fault.

'Well, did you know, Zoe, that you have a bicornuate uterus?'

'A what?' she asked.

'It's heart shaped. About four in a thousand women have them. Baby MacGinley is implanted on one side, but the other doesn't have anything in it, so thinks you are due a period. This is what caused the bleeding. It's likely it will keep going for a while, so don't be too concerned.'

'What does this mean for the pregnancy?' she asked.

'It's still early days, so difficult to say. Some women do have issues such as preterm or breech babies, but others go through life never knowing they have this condition.'

Still early days. Issues. Preterm. Breech.

He'd done this to her, and he could do it again.

Zoe wanted to speak to her mum, so Rory gave her some privacy, leaving her in the hospital cafe with a pot of tea and a slice of cake.

He then stood outside under a grey sky, the crushing weight of responsibility pressing down on him. He was used to putting his big feet in situations, but now his big cock had almost lost them their child.

Taking out his phone, he rang Charlie. He didn't care what time it was in LA. He needed his best mate.

Charlie picked up just as Rory was expecting it to go to voicemail.

'This had better be good,' he said, his voice gravelly. 'I've got a photoshoot in the morning and need my beauty sleep.'

'I need some advice.'

'Huh? No attempt at a witty comeback? No slagging off *Cosmopolitan's* Sexiest Man of the Year?'

'Not this time.'

There was a pause.

'Fuck, okay. Hang on.'

Rory heard a slapping sound.

'Right,' said Charlie, sounding much more alert. 'I've deployed stage one of waking myself up. How can I help?'

'I'm at the hospital. Zoe's nine weeks pregnant and had a massive bleed last night. The baby's okay, but it's all my fault.'

There was silence, then the sound of Charlie slapping his face again.

'That's a lot to unpack,' he began. 'First up, congrats. Knew you had it in you. Second, is Zoe okay? Third, can I tell Valentina? And fourth, how the actual fuck is it your fault?'

Rory's heart felt too heavy for his chest. 'Zoe doesn't have to stay in the hospital and says she's fine, but who really knows? You can tell Valentina, but please keep it from her family or the whole bloody world will know.' He sighed. 'And it's my fault because it happened when we were having sex.'

'Is that what the doctor said?'

'Not in so many words, but Zoe's got a heart-shaped uterus which can make a pregnancy risky. And...'

'Ye-es?'

'You know,' Rory replied, testily, 'I've got a big cock.'

Charlie snorted. 'Not as big as mine, mate.'

'Bollocks.'

'They're bigger too.'

'Fuck off, this is serious.'

'So, why do you need my advice? Do you need me to hook you up with Hollywood's finest plastic surgeon for a penis reduction?'

'Don't be a twat.'

'Can't help it. It's hard-wired into my DNA. And anyway, I think Valentina finds it cute.'

Rory thought about Charlie's fiancée. He was glad his friend had finally found someone who truly loved him.

'You still there?'

'Yeah,' Rory replied. 'I need to ask for your advice.'

'So you said.'

'But I don't want you to laugh or take the piss.'

'Mate, you know I can't promise that.'

'Fine—'

'Hang on. I'll be serious. Come on, out with it.'

Rory sighed. 'Okay, here's the deal. Pregnancy is less fun than five days in a foxhole with food poisoning. Zoe's knackered, feels sick the whole time and the only time she feels okay is when she's asleep, sometimes when she eats, or if she's having an orgasm. There's no fucking way my cock is going anywhere near her until the baby's out, so I need some alternatives.'

'Fuck my life. Your fingers? Your tongue?'

'If I'm involved, she'll want it all.'

'The earl's sausage as well as the side dishes?'

Rory raised his eyes to the heavens. 'You are such a dick.'

'Yes, but right now, the problem is *your* dick. Have you spoken to Zoe about all this?'

'No.'

'Don't you think you should?'

'I don't want to. She's overwhelmed with being pregnant and her plans for bloody fucking Christmas.'

'Is that the song by The Pogues and Kirsty MacColl?'

Rory ignored him. 'I'm trying to keep it together for her right now. She's the one with the hard job. She doesn't need my bullshit. There's plenty to take me away from the cabin, so I need to get her some, erm, toys...'

'You don't have any already?'

'What? Fuck no.'

'Seriously? Mate, you're missing a trick. They're not competition, they're fun. A rabbit is your friend, not your foe.'

'A rabbit? What the fuck are you on about? I want a vibrator, not another pet.'

Charlie's laugh was so loud, Rory had to hold the phone away from his ear.

'Mate, you're fucking priceless!'

'Look, are you going to help me or not?'

The sound of Charlie slapping himself echoed down the line, and the laughter stopped.

'Ahem. Yes, Mr Charlie Hamilton is here to save the day. Now, let's start with specifications.'

❀ 5 ❀

July. Twelve weeks + four

Rory hated hospitals. In his life, they were never associated with anything pleasant. During his army days, he'd had the misfortune to be blown up in Afghanistan. He was one of the lucky ones, keeping all his limbs as well as his life. But lying in a hospital bed with too much time to think had taken its toll.

He was confident he'd dealt with his PTSD a long time ago, but every time he smelled the mix of cleaning fluid and cabbage, or heard the squeak of rubber shoes on a linoleum floor, forgotten feelings and emotions woke from their graves to stalk him.

But he had to bite the bullet. Zoe was booked in for multiple appointments and he was going to be there for every single one. So far, pregnancy seemed like a never-ending ride on a decrepit rollercoaster after drinking five bottles of Buckfast.

Zoe was still feeling sick the whole time, her bladder had

the capacity of a teacup, she was perpetually exhausted, and her emotions had more bounce than a bungee cord. Maybe this was why his parents only had him. God only knew how Fiona always appeared so bonny.

And despite his best intentions and how many hours a day he worked to relieve Zoe's workload, she seemed unable to step off the bridge of the good ship Christmas and let him shoulder more of the responsibility.

If Rory had his way, the celebrations would require less input than a pedalo on a boating lake. However, Zoe's version of Christmas was a cruise liner crossed with a container ship. The only good thing was that she hadn't seemed to notice they'd stopped having sex.

Charlie had come through for him with a shopping list of vibrators long enough to stock a sex shop. Rory had no idea there were so many permutations. They vibrated, they pulsed, they had ultrasonic waves, they sucked, they blew, they had two heads, three heads, ears, rattling balls. Some were even remote controlled. Rory thought he knew what sex involved, but it was clear he was a caveman living in a sci-fi world and hadn't yet got with the programme. He'd ordered a selection that were mainly external, ensuring anything that would be penetrating her was half the size of his cock, then put them through the castle accounts under 'hospitality and entertainment'.

Red-faced, he'd presented them to Zoe one morning, explaining that he wasn't going to be around much. The embarrassment turned into relief when it seemed they were doing the trick. And when he thought she might initiate any intimacy, he made an excuse to leave the cabin. There was no way he was going to let his selfish desires risk her health or the baby's.

However, sitting in the consultation room at the hospital, it appeared his cunning plan had not been entirely effective.

'Everything's alright then?' Zoe asked the elderly midwife.

'Oh yes, dear. You're now into your second trimester. Your baby is fully formed and just needs to cook.'

'So, it's okay to have sex?'

The woman peered at Zoe over the top of her glasses. 'Why, yes, dear. Are you not indulging in marital relations at present?' She looked keenly at Rory, as if he was to blame.

'No. My husband refuses to have sex with me.'

What?

'Oh,' replied the midwife. She took her glasses off to give him the full force of her glare. 'And why is that?'

'Um, we do. I mean, er, you do have...' Rory broke off and pulled the collar of his shirt away from his neck. Why were hospitals always so bloody hot? 'I've, er, ensured that you are, ahem, satisfied,' he concluded, extremely aware of how *dis*satisfied both his wife and the midwife currently appeared to be.

Zoe swivelled in her chair to face him. 'Yes, but none of those instances involve you or your penis going anywhere near my body. And anyway, what about *your* needs?'

'My needs?' *What do they have to do with anything?*

'Yes, Rory. I want to give *you* pleasure. I want your cock in—'

He coughed loudly. Jesus Christ, did she not realise Mrs Doubtfire was taking notes?

'We're not going to have sex until after the birth. I don't want to hurt you or the baby,' he replied testily.

'What?' Zoe screeched. 'Is that what all the sex toys are about?'

The midwife chuckled. 'Mr MacGinley, this is a common concern, but entirely unfounded. I'm positive your penis is no different from any other man's. Besides, the female vagina can accommodate pretty much anything, and the cervix and mucous plug protect the baby.'

Zoe had a dangerous glint in her eye. 'See, your penis is as average as the next man's.'

'But what about Zoe's bleed three weeks ago? The risk?'

'Mr MacGinley. Your wife stopped passing blood over a week ago, and even if it continued, normal intercourse is perfectly safe. Your penis—'

'Will you *please* stop talking about my penis?' Sweat was trickling down his back. Fucking hell, women could be terrifying. Thank god his mother was on the other side of the Atlantic.

'Maybe...' Zoe replied, crossing her arms. The movement pushed her breasts together. They'd been getting bigger over the last few weeks.

Rory tore his gaze away and focused on the little old lady, who had a naughtier glint in her eye than his wife's.

'Look, are you sure I'm not going to cause any harm?'

'There are no guarantees, Mr MacGinley, but it's extremely unlikely. If you are truly concerned about your penis, I can make you an appointment with the urologist, Doctor Payne?'

Zoe snorted with laughter.

Rory stood, the chair pushing back with a screech. 'That will not be necessary.'

'Marvellous. I'll see you in a few weeks.' She handed Zoe her maternity notes with a wink. 'Have fun, Mrs MacGinley.'

ZOE SKIPPED OUT OF RAIGMORE HOSPITAL, SINGING 'LET'S Talk About Sex' by Salt-N-Pepa. By the time they'd reached the car park, she was body-popping to 'I Want Your Sex' by George Michael. Back in the truck, she started crooning 'Let's Get It On' by Marvin Gaye.

Rory rested his head back and sighed. 'Did you enjoy that?'

'Might have done,' she replied, stretching her arms over her head and pushing out her chest. Rory swallowed and tried not to stare at her breasts.

She put her hand on his trousers. His cock was already hard.

'How is your penis?' she asked innocently. 'It feels a bit stiff. Does it need a massage?'

Closing his eyes, he groaned. 'Fuck's sake, Zoe.'

'Rory, please can we go home and put your definitely not average cock in my perfectly safe and normal vagina? Pretty, pretty please?'

He sighed. 'If you're sure?'

Her response was to unlace her boots.

'What are you doing?'

'Getting ready. I want to have sex the moment we get home.'

Rory started the engine and eased out of the space. He could do this.

By the time they turned down the track to the cabin, Zoe was naked from the waist up. However, as they rounded the final bend, Rory suddenly slammed the truck in reverse.

They were not alone.

'Who the fuck was that?' Zoe asked as she hastily redressed.

'God knows,' he replied. 'But I'd rather they didn't see your spectacular breasts or my "perfectly average penis".'

'Well, whoever they are, let's get rid of them quickly.'

As soon as Zoe was decent, Rory eased the truck back along the track. The car parked outside the cabin was a big black SUV with tinted windows.

No one got out to greet them.

'Dudes!'

Rory had been glad of the sex reprieve, but now his heart sank.

There, in the distance, walking up the hill from the loch towards them, hand in hand with Bandit at their side, was his mother and her much younger husband: Hollywood superstar, and all-round fruit-loop, Brad Bauer.

'Promise you'll behave,' Zoe said.

Rory was silent.

'Rory!' she hissed.

He grunted.

'Rory grumpy-pants MacGinley. You have less than a minute to get it together. You will smile. You will make pleasant conversation. And you will not lose your shit if Brad calls you—'

'Son!'

Zoe's nails dug into Rory's arm, the pain a welcome distraction. His father, who'd died three years previously, had been a domineering bully, who'd sent Rory off to boarding school in England aged seven.

Rory was not in the market for a replacement father figure, certainly not one only a few years older than himself who drank smoothies for breakfast with the consistency and colour of something scraped off the bottom of the loch.

Zoe strode forward. 'Barbara, Brad, what an unexpected surprise.'

His mother air-kissed her and Brad stared at her stomach.

'Where is it?' he asked.

'Bradley, dear,' replied his mother with the kind of tone reserved for toddlers. 'We've been over this already. Zoe won't show for at least another month, maybe longer.'

Brad looked disappointed, but immediately bounced back, hugging Zoe. 'Babe, we're so excited!'

Rory stalked over and Brad let go of Zoe and grabbed him in a bear hug. 'There you are. Bring it in, man. Bring it in!'

Rory patted Brad's back awkwardly until relieved by his mother.

'Congratulations, darling,' she said, leaving a good six inches between her air kiss and his cheek. 'Although I'm not sure what all *this* is about,' she said, waving at his beard. 'Are you planning to play Joseph in the nativity this year?'

'Zoe wants me to be Santa.'

Barbara looked appalled. 'Aren't you a little young? And I didn't think you even *liked* the concept of Father Christmas?'

That was true. The idea of a strange man entering his bedroom when he was asleep had given Rory nightmares as a child.

'I thought it might bring more people in if they knew it was the earl in the suit,' said Zoe.

His mother sniffed. 'Very well, although he'll have to work on his fireside manner.'

'Why are you here?' Rory asked, as pleasantly as he could manage.

'Rory!'

'It's alright, dear,' his mother said to Zoe with a smile. 'I know it's a little unexpected. We just wanted to congratulate you on reaching the second stage of your gestational journey, and offer our assistance.'

'How did you know we were in the second trimester?' Rory asked. Did he need to sweep the cabin for bugs?

'My shaman, dude!' said Brad. 'He's got his third eye on you.'

Fuck's sake. 'Shaman?'

'Yeah, Jesus.'

'Christ,' Rory muttered.

'No, man, his surname's de la Cruz.'

'Darling,' Barbara interjected, laying her hand on Brad's arm. 'You really should pronounce his name "Hay*suss*".'

'But, babe! "Jesus" sounds way sicker.'

'Bradley,' his mother said, in a tone Rory knew was a warning.

'Yes, Countess,' Brad replied, standing to attention.

Fuck my life. They really *did* have that dynamic going on.

'So!' Zoe said brightly. 'Your shaman?'

'Yeah, man! I met him at an Ayahuasca retreat. He's been watching you for me. That's how we know how far along you are.'

'That,' continued Barbara, 'and some basic mathematics.'

'What else has Jesús said about my pregnancy?' asked Zoe, her hands creeping protectively over her belly.

Rory stepped closer to her side.

'You're having a boy, and I'm going to be at the birth,' Brad replied.

Silence.

'It *is* a little bracing this afternoon, and we have been waiting a while,' said his mother. 'Shall we adjourn inside for a cup of tea?'

INSIDE THE CABIN, ZOE AND RORY SAT ACROSS THE DINING table from Barbara and Brad. Zoe chatted happily with Barbara, appearing to have made the decision to ignore Brad's proclamation for the insanity it was.

Rory, on the other hand, was engaged in a desperate battle to subdue his inner caveman. He thought he'd come to terms with his mother marrying the Hollywood star, however imagining Brad present whilst Zoe gave birth made the green mist descend and his caveman Hulk out.

'So, Zoe dear, how are you feeling?'

Considering how much his mother had hated Zoe in the past, this pleasant side of her was unnerving.

'Still very tired and a bit sick, to be honest, but okay, I suppose? I don't really know what to expect.'

'Well, Bradley and I don't want to tread on your toes, but we are very keen to help in any way. Especially with the logistics.'

'Logistics?'

'Yes, we'll draft the official announcement and handle the press release. I've already provisionally booked a room at the family's private hospital in Edinburgh for the delivery, and I'm thrilled to say I've already researched the correct name for the baby.'

'The name?' Zoe's voice went up a register.

'Of course you won't know the family tradition, but it's terribly complicated. It took me hours with a genealogist to ensure Rory was named correctly. However, Bradley took me to the Scottish Highland Institute of Tartan Excellence in Los Angeles, and they did it on a computer in a matter of minutes.'

Barbara took a piece of paper from her bag and put it on the table in front of them. 'No need to thank me, dear. It was my pleasure.'

They stared at the printout.

'Stuart Uisdan Murdock Oengus,' said Zoe, faintly.

'Yes, but Uisdan is pronounced Ooshdan,' said Barbara. 'And Oengus has more of an "uh" sound, like fungus.'

'Barbara Euphemia Grissel Anabald?'

'I know you're carrying the heir,' his mother continued.' But just in case, I've included the correct name for a girl.'

'*Barbara?*'

'Yes, the first-born female is always named after the paternal grandmother.'

There was a short silence, then Zoe started to laugh.

When Zoe was in a very stressful situation, she burst into hysterical laughter. But it wasn't funny to her; it was panicked, painful and uncontrollable.

Rory held her shaking hands in his. 'Look at me. Breathe with me.'

Her whole body was convulsing as she hyperventilated, desperately trying to draw in air.

'Aha, ahaha, ahahahaha!'

'In through your nose, out through your mouth. You're okay.'

Barbara was looking askance at Zoe, and Brad stared at her with undisguised interest. Rory made a mental note to ensure her condition never made it into one of his films.

After a minute, she got her breathing back under control, and he passed her a handkerchief.

'Thank you.' Zoe wiped her eyes, blew her nose, then took a long breath in and out.

'Barbara,' she said firmly. 'I'm extremely appreciative of the thought and time that has gone into your research. However, the name of our child will be decided by Rory and myself. The fate of Scotland doesn't depend on us following this particular tradition.'

'But—'

'Babe!' said Brad excitedly. 'They can go with Jesus's vision!'

No, we fucking won't.

'Hay*suss*, Bradley, Hay*suss*.'

'It came to him during ceremony,' Brad continued.

Rory squeezed Zoe's hand, trying to reassure her that whatever wind of insanity was about to blow their way, she could close the door on it.

'Rob Roy Macbeth for a dude, or Heather Loch Leary for a dudette!'

'No,' said Rory.

'And I'm going to give birth in Raigmore hospital in Inverness,' added Zoe.

'Very well,' his mother replied, her lips thinning.

Rory knew just how much of an effort she was making to be nice.

Brad deflated for a moment, then recovered like a puppy distracted by a new toy. 'We got you some books!'

His mother took two books from her bag and gave them to Zoe.

One had a picture of a baby and was titled 'The New Contented Little Baby Book'. The other had an elaborately illustrated cover with children and animals and was called 'The Nourishing Traditions Book of Baby & Child Care'.

'Bradley's contribution has a more alternative approach to proceedings, but, as you said, this is *your* pregnancy and you must make the right decisions for you.'

Zoe pushed her chair back, her eyes filling with tears as she embraced his mother. 'Thank you, Barbara.'

Barbara looked startled at the sudden affection, patting Zoe stiffly on the back.

'You guys!' cried Brad, enveloping them both in a hug. 'Bring it in!'

Zoe pulled away.

'Bradley!' snapped Barbara.

He sat back.

Barbara got to her feet. 'We'll stay at the castle tonight, then take the jet back tomorrow afternoon. This is just a flying visit to check in with you both.' She paused and fiddled with the clasp on her bag. 'Unfortunately, due to Bradley's commitments, we may not make it back before the birth.'

Brad stood and put his arms around her. 'Babe,' he said, softly.

She gave him a little nod, then lifted her head. 'Bradley, the castle.'

He straightened. 'Yes, Countess.'

❧ 6 ❧

July. Twelve weeks + five

Zoe never knew how fascinating a tiny sleeping human could be until she met Fiona's daughter. Even though she knew a pregnant belly contained a baby, now Isla was on the other side of her friend's tummy, the whole process seemed completely unreal.

Fiona had given birth two days earlier, and this was the first time they'd met the latest addition to the Sinclair household. Rory had held Isla as if she was an unstable bomb for thirty seconds, before going outside to play football in the garden with Duncan and Liam.

'I know I probably sound like I'm mental or something, but now she's here it's like part of me doesn't understand where she came from,' Zoe said quietly. 'It's like you've performed some kind of magic trick.'

Fiona smiled. 'I know what you mean. Ten minutes after I squeezed this little munchkin out of my vagina, I wondered if the stork had brought her.'

Zoe clenched her thighs together. 'How was it? The birth?'

'It was fine. Much quicker than with Liam. That lasted a week.'

'A week?' Isla stirred and Zoe rocked her back to sleep.

'Yeah,' Fiona continued. 'I was bloody exhausted. I was in and out of Raigmore more times than a sex addict doing the Hokey Cokey.'

'Why didn't they let you stay?'

'Because I wasn't dilated enough and they didn't want to waste a bed. They want you to come in as late as possible.'

'But how will I *know* when I'm ready?'

Fiona puffed out her cheeks. 'Honestly, Zo, every labour is different. Just don't even think about calling the midwife until it's been a few hours of contractions so regular and hard you think you might pass out.'

'What?'

'Shit! Sorry, love, that sounded fucking awful. It'll be fine. I promise. Just don't go in until you can't hold a conversation. You don't want to do that car journey more than once.'

'I could have a home birth like you did with Isla?'

'You could. It was a million times better than the hospital. But at the same time, I knew what to expect. And when I was pregnant with Liam, I had to think of Duncan. He would have supported me, of course, if I'd wanted a home birth, but I didn't want him silently freaking out. What does Rory think?'

'We haven't discussed it yet. It all seems so far away. I'd like to be at home for most of it at least. Mum had a really long labour with me as well, and I'd rather be in the cabin than in a hospital ward.'

They sat in a companionable silence as Isla slept on, listening to the sounds of Duncan playing football with Liam in the back garden.

'He's not going back this time,' said Fiona.

'Duncan?'

Fiona nodded.

'Because of what happened to your dad?'

'Yes. I didn't want to tell you because I didn't want you to worry, but I kept imagining Mum being pregnant with Jamie when Dad died out on the rigs. That level of stress is just not worth it. And anyway, I've really struggled with this pregnancy, and don't want to have to deal with two kids on my own for two weeks out of four.'

'Are you going to be okay for money?'

'For a while, we should be. We've been saving for years, so we have enough to upgrade to our forever home and keep ourselves fed for a few months at least. Dunc can always pick up work as an electrician. We'll be fine.'

October. Twenty-eight weeks

WITH ONE LOOK FROM HIS WIFE, RORY KNEW HE WAS IN trouble.

He'd returned to the cabin to find Zoe, naked from the waist down, washing clothes in the sink. It couldn't have been another bleed as she looked mad, not sad.

'What's happened?'

She pointed a soapy finger at him. '*You* happened, Rory.'

'Um.' He racked his brains to try and think what he'd done.

'The toilet?'

Fuck. He'd forgotten to tell her.

'You baby-proofed the bloody loo and didn't tell me! You know I have the bladder control of a small dog after drinking a pint of builder's tea,' she ranted. 'I tried for thirty seconds to work it out, failed, and pissed myself before I could find a bucket.'

'Shit.'

'Luckily it wasn't that, or I'd be even madder.'

'I'm sorry.'

'Rory, our baby isn't going to be born till next year and won't be mobile for at least six months after that. You've got a phone line sorted to the cabin now. That's the most important thing done. You need to stop baby-proofing everything. The Rayburn doesn't need to be fenced off, the furniture doesn't need to be wrapped in foam, and the bloody toilet seat doesn't need more security than Fort Knox.'

'Okay.'

'Is that an "okay, I'll put away the bubble wrap", or an "okay, let's placate the pregnant woman"?'

'I'll put baby-proofing on hold.'

'And sort the loo seat. I need to go again before we leave for the next scan.'

An hour later, Rory stared at the moving black-and-white image. This was what he needed to protect. His wife had not accidentally swallowed a basketball. A tiny, defenceless human was inside her belly.

The sonographer laughed. 'Och, you're a wee wriggler.'

'I think they're playing football,' said Zoe. 'That or break-dancing.'

Football's for plebs. Rugby's a real man's game. His father's words stole into the room like an icy draft, and he gripped Zoe's hand tighter.

'Did you want to know the sex?' the sonographer asked.

Zoe glanced his way and raised her eyebrows as if checking he hadn't changed his mind from their last appointment.

He shook his head.

'No thanks,' she replied. 'We're going to keep it a surprise. Even though everyone thinks it's a boy, even me.'

Rory's heart thudded inside his chest. *Please, not a boy.* He rarely thought about his father. But ever since that second blue line had appeared on the pregnancy test, long-forgotten memories from his childhood had woken to slash at his heart and confidence.

'Well, not long to go now,' said the sonographer with a beaming smile. 'Next year you'll have your answer.'

Fear swelled inside him, squeezing each breath. Rory knew Zoe would be the best mum, but could he avoid being like his father? He tried to banish the thoughts with logic, but they still followed him whether he was awake or asleep, pushing all his buttons with laser-pointed accuracy. And he didn't want to burden Zoe with his fears, as she was exhausted and overwhelmed.

Organising the perfect Christmas for the castle had stretched them to the limit, and even though they'd brought in Duncan to help with running the estate, it still wasn't enough.

At least the festival of light was now underway. The previous night, the rain had held off, and the gardens were packed as people wandered a trail through different light displays. Even though it was only late October, the local choir had sung carols, and everyone had been merry on mulled wine or hot chocolate.

'Can we stop and get a copy of *The Courier* before we head home?' Zoe asked as they left the hospital. 'I want to see the pictures from last night.'

Rory nodded. Thank god it had gone off without a hitch.

. . .

TEN MINUTES LATER, RORY KNEW HE SHOULDN'T HAVE counted his chickens.

'No!' cried Zoe. 'No, no, no, no!'

His fingers clenched around the steering wheel. 'What's wrong?'

'How did I miss this? Fuck! Rory, was this some kind of joke between you and Duncan?'

'What? What's a joke?'

Zoe started crying.

Fuck! Rory scanned the road for a safe place to stop. 'Hang on.'

Swerving into a layby, he cut the engine and reached for her hand. 'What's happened?'

Zoe passed him the paper.

The entirety of the front page was taken up with a report from the festival of light.

'Earl balls up at family event!' screamed the headline, and underneath, above the fold, was a photo of one of the displays. It was a small temple built by one of Rory's ancestors after returning from his Grand Tour in the seventeenth century. Circular, with thick stone columns that supported the roof, at the base of each column were a pair of large granite balls.

Rory had never noticed the phallic nature of the structure. It was just another part of the castle. So he'd wrapped the columns and balls in fairy lights with Duncan, too busy meeting the deadline for either of them to look at their work with a critical eye.

But now, illuminated in the darkness, it was obvious what it looked like.

Once again, the Earl of Kinloch seems determined to display the alleged dimensions of his personal endowments in public... This event is marketed at families, but with the amount of alcohol present and this lewd and immature display, people should think twice before attend-

ing... Another cheap publicity stunt by a man who supported the histor-ically inaccurate and culturally offensive film, Braveheart 2... "It's disgusting," an anonymous witness stated. "I had to explain to my grandson exactly why people were laughing so much."

Rory sighed.

The article didn't mention the wreath-making workshops, the carol singing, the kiddies nose-deep in hot chocolate with whipped cream and marshmallows. He'd been there from opening to closing and all he'd seen were happy faces. Rory didn't give two shits about the article, but he gave every shit about his wife's happiness, and right now, she was still crying.

'This is all my fault,' she hiccupped. 'I should have noticed. And now everything's ruined.'

Rory rubbed his thumb over the back of her hand. If this had happened when Zoe was less stressed and exhausted, she would have laughed it off, gleefully exclaiming about the extra publicity and putting a link to the article on the castle website. But now, she seemed devastated.

'It's not your fault,' he said. 'It's mine for not noticing. This article is bullshit. You saw how much everyone loved it. You've done something amazing.'

'It's a disaster. We need to take those lights down.'

'Fuck, no. Remember when you told me that all publicity is good publicity? I'm going to get Duncan to help me rig up more lights at the top of the columns. I want it to look like they're ejaculating onto the roof.'

Zoe snorted and his heart lifted.

'Maybe we can put a giant inflatable baby on the top?' he continued. 'Say it's an art installation celebrating your pregnancy?'

Zoe's tears were turning into laughs. 'Don't you dare, Rory MacGinley.'

'And how about we start serving those "Earl sausages" the

butcher created last year? We can get the bakery to produce a "Zoe roll" to go with them.'

She shrieked with laughter and his heart soared. If he could make her smile, everything would be okay.

❧

November. Thirty-two weeks + four

THIRD TIME LUCKY.

Zoe slowly typed 'Roryissexy' into the password box.

Access denied.

Feeling the first flickers of panic, she tried 'Roryissexy69', 'manbear69', and 'IlikebigScotsandIcannotlie'.

None of them worked.

She cradled her bump. *Breathe slowly in and out. Stress is bad for the baby. A crisis is an opportunity. Christmas is going to be perfect. You've got a month. A MONTH? FUCK!*

The castle website was their point of contact with the public, and Zoe was locked out.

Duncan was gazing at her with concern from across the estate office. 'Everything okay?'

'I can't get into the website.'

'Can you reset the password?'

'No. I can't do anything. Have you been in the back end at all?'

He raised his hands. 'No way. That's your domain. I just do whatever Rory tells me.'

She raised an eyebrow. 'You mean the jobs he doesn't want to do?'

Duncan grinned. 'Fine by me. I'd rather be inside than out in all that.'

Zoe glanced at the icy rain hurling itself at the windows.

Winter was beginning to bite. Having Duncan working for them was a blessing *and* a curse. It helped with some of Rory's workload, but meant they hardly saw each other. Pregnancy hormones were making her hornier than ever, but a desk quickie was now impossible, and by the time they both returned to the cabin at night, she was too exhausted.

Her perfect Christmas was also not going according to plan. The bad weather meant lower numbers for the light festival, they were haemorrhaging money on electricity, and the friends of Brad who were hiring the castle over Christmas were more demanding than the love child of Madonna and Kim Jong-un. All ticket sales for the ceilidh were going through the website, and now she couldn't get in.

'Do you think it's been hacked?' Duncan asked.

'Good lord, no,' she bluffed. 'We're not the Pentagon. I'll ring customer support and see what's going on.'

Five minutes later, the enormity of the situation sank in. Zoe had missed updating the site's plug-ins, and a bot had gained access. As well as locking her out, all the financial details of anyone who'd bought a ticket to the ceilidh had been compromised. It was a total disaster.

DUNCAN WAS ON THE PHONE WORKING HIS WAY THROUGH the list of people who'd purchased tickets when Rory arrived, his cheeks red from the cold and his wet hair dripping onto the parquet floor.

'What can I do to help?' he asked.

'Dunc's ringing anyone who's bought a ticket and I'm on a live chat with a security company. We can't risk selling anything through the website, so we're going to have to go old school. Posters up everywhere and tickets on the door or sold through the post office. Can I leave that job to you?'

He nodded. 'Date, time, location, price. Anything else?'

'Live band. And make sure the posters scream Christmas and party.'

Rory looked unsure. 'Any specific instructions? Do you want to see the design?'

Zoe was trying to keep her focus on the online chat. There was no headspace left for another job.

'We don't have time. Just tell them to keep it simple. Red, holly, baubles. Anything that tells people it's a party and they're going to have fun.'

He nodded again and took out his phone.

HALF AN HOUR LATER, THE WEBSITE WAS UNDER CONTROL and Zoe joined Duncan in contacting anyone whose details might have been compromised. In the background, she could hear Rory fighting to keep his cool.

'It's a *ceilidh*. A party... Red, holly, balloons, the usual Christmas stuff... What? Yes, it's a party. A ceilidh... A party for ceilidh? What? The party *is* the ceilidh...' He ran a hand into his wet hair, grabbing clumps and tugging them away from his scalp. 'Look. Just keep it simple. Ceilidh, Christmas, Kinloch Castle. As long as people know where to come and when, and how much it costs, I don't care what the final design looks like.'

Rory looked over at Zoe as if seeking her reassurance with this decision.

She nodded.

'And we'll pay extra for you to put the posters up around Inverness and the villages around Kinloch,' Rory continued. 'You can send the tickets directly to Morag MacDougall at Kinloch post office.'

Zoe finished her call as Rory ended his. He opened his arms, and she was drawn into his warmth and security.

'Thank you,' she said into his chest.

'How can something that simple be so hard?' he grumbled.

'Did they not know what a ceilidh was?'

'They weren't Scottish, so I presume not. And it sounded like there was a TV in the background playing Formula One, so I think that's where their attention was.'

'We could always try another company?'

He shuddered. 'No way. One call like that is enough.' He hugged her tighter. 'Do you need anything else, or can I go back to repairing a fence in the rain?'

'You'd rather do that than stay with me?' she teased.

'If Duncan wasn't here, I'd stay,' he whispered in her ear as he nuzzled her curly hair. 'You could always come with me?'

'I can't. There's too much to do.' She sighed. 'There's always too much to do.'

7

December first. Thirty-four weeks

It didn't matter that there was a national mistletoe shortage. It didn't matter that the paying guests due in three weeks were impossible to please. It didn't matter that her bump was so big, it was getting difficult to tie her boots. Zoe was so horny she couldn't think straight.

Maybe it was the hormones, or perhaps orgasms were the best form of stress relief. But right now, she couldn't get enough, and her schedule hardly allowed for any.

Leaving Duncan in the estate office, she waddled out of the castle to her truck, dialling Rory when she was inside.

'Everything okay?' he asked.

'Where are you?'

'The quarry. You alright?'

'I need you.'

'Can Duncan help? The charges are about to go off here.'

'I *need*, need you. So no, Duncan most definitely cannot help.'

'Ah.'

There was a pause. In the background, Zoe heard the quarry siren announcing the forthcoming explosion. She was sure Rory didn't really need to be there, but she also knew how much he liked blowing things up.

'What about Bob?' he asked.

'Which one?'

'Fuck, I don't know. Bullet Bob?'

'Out of batteries.'

'Bunny Bob?'

'Basil found it and ate the ears off.'

'Oh. Bedtime Bob?'

'On charge and won't be ready for a few hours.'

'Back-up Bob?'

'Broke through overuse and is now Bandit's favourite chew toy.'

'Big Bob?'

'You're Big Bob.'

There was another pause. 'You heading back to the cabin?'

'Yes.'

'I'll be there in ten.'

By the time Rory entered the cabin, Zoe was on the bed, extremely hot and bothered.

'Let me give you a hand,' he said with a grin as he toed off his boots.

'Bloody big bump and bloody stupid socks!' she yelled.

Kneeling front of her, he pulled them off and massaged her aching feet. 'You should be resting more.'

Zoe ignored him. She felt guilty enough for taking this time away from work. 'Oh, my god that feels so good.'

Rory stroked up her calves, kneading the muscles. 'Would you like a massage and a nap?'

Her eyes snapped open. 'Rory MacGinley. I am so horny I could combust. The only massage I need right now is an internal one. Get naked. Now.'

He saluted her, then tugged his shirt off.

Zoe swallowed as she watched the rippling muscles of his torso. She must have been Mother Teresa in a former life to have been gifted Rory in this one. As his cock sprang free, she grabbed it greedily.

'Gimme, gimme.'

'I thought this was meant to be about you,' he said, his breath hitching as she stroked and squeezed him.

'I like Big Bob and I cannot lie,' she replied before sucking him deep.

'Zoe! Fuck!'

He tried to move, but she held him firmly, her free hand tugging the weight of his balls. She loved the way she could reduce this huge strong man to a shaking mess.

'Zoe, seriously, it's been too long, I'm—'

She released him with a pop.

Rory gritted his teeth, the tendons in his neck strained. His breath rushed out with a whoosh as he regained control, then his arctic blue eyes fixed her with a stare that could melt diamonds.

He pointed to the headboard. 'Get up there and hold on tight.'

Zoe scooted back, kneeling up and facing away from him. She moaned as his hand cupped her from behind, running his fingers through the slickness of her arousal. Pregnancy made everything feel fuller, more sensitive. Rory bit her neck and thrust two fingers inside.

'Yes!'

She rocked back against the hardness of his shaft, already so close to coming. Holding her breast with his other hand, Rory pinched and tugged her nipple. Zoe gasped as sensation sparked, sending shocks of light through her.

His thumb found her clit, and she bucked frantically into his hand. He growled into her neck and the vibrations sent her over the edge, her muscles convulsing as her orgasm hit. Rory held her tightly, continuing to nip, pinch and rub every point of pleasure as she fell apart in his arms.

As her breath slowed, he pulled his fingers from her.

'Rory,' she whined.

He pressed his cock between her thighs and she squeezed around it.

'Is this what you want?' he asked, his voice gravelly and deep.

'Yes, yes, yes!' One orgasm had barely scratched the surface of her need.

He moved the thick length back and forward. 'And how do you want it, Zoe?'

His body covered hers, his hands roaming over her breasts, her belly.

'Hard,' she gasped.

He nudged her knees wider, and she angled her bottom up. The feel of the fat head of his shaft nudging into her was the most exquisite relief. He moved slowly as she adjusted to his size, brushing his fingers over her clit and sending more urgent rushes of pleasure through her to pop and fizz across her skin.

'More, Rory. I need more.'

He pushed deeper, and she wriggled back against him until he filled her completely. Zoe sighed with pleasure. Her body, mind and soul were full of Rory and she could never get enough.

He withdrew slowly, then pushed forward. His pace was slow and steady, building the fire inside her.

'Faster, Rory. Harder.'

Gripping the headboard, she met his thrusts with her own, but he was still holding back.

'Wait,' he growled.

He held her hip steady with one hand, the other teasing her clit. 'One more orgasm won't be enough.'

She whimpered.

'Touch your breasts. I've got you.'

Releasing her hands from the end of the bed, Zoe tugged her nipples.

Rory rolled her clit between his fingers and thumb.

'Oh my god, oh my god,' she moaned.

His cock continued to move. In, out. In, out. The pressure was rising. Pleasure bubbled and boiled inside her. Her breaths came faster as he rocked her higher.

'Yes, yes, yes!'

He pinched her clit, and she detonated with a scream. Thrusting faster, he chased her orgasm over the cliff as she cried out, again and again.

The sensations rolled on as he thrust harder, and she gasped. 'Rory! I'm going to come again!'

He pulled her body closer, angling her head so he could kiss her, his hips snapping faster. Another climax barrelled through, stealing her breath and filling her head with stars.

Rory wrenched his head from hers as he lost control, crying her name, his hips jerking as he came inside her.

She slumped forward and he eased her down to the bed, cradling her as she lay on her side.

'I love you so much,' she mumbled.

'I love you too,' he murmured, nuzzling into her hair.

He held her close as she drifted off to sleep.

R ORY SANDED THE PIECE OF WOOD UNTIL IT WAS AS SMOOTH as silk. He'd left Zoe to rest and returned to his workshop to finish the crib he was making for their baby. It had various iterations and was able to fit flush with the edge of the bed, as well as expand to stand on its own.

He'd declined the offer of a suite of nursery furniture from his mother and Brad. Rory didn't want anything he hadn't made, and he was sure the baby didn't need more furniture than the entire east wing of the castle.

Both he and Zoe wanted to live in the cabin for as long as possible after the baby was born. However, Rory knew someday they would have to leave it behind and make the castle their permanent home.

The imposing building still held echoes of his father. The thump of his boots, the bark of his voice, the crack of his whip against the stonework. The only way Rory could think to avoid being like him was to make sure everything he did was the polar opposite of his father's brutish behaviour. But no matter how Rory tried to reassure himself with logic, fear still crept in.

Pulling out his phone, he rang Charlie.

His best mate picked up almost immediately. 'Charlie's Confidential Crisis line, the proprietor speaking.'

Rory shook his head. 'You're such a twat.'

'I know,' Charlie replied happily. 'What's up and how's Zoe doing?'

'Up and down. Stressed about everything we've got to do for Christmas, whilst growing a human. Thank fuck we don't have to do the whole pregnancy thing.'

'Valentina wants about a million kids, so I hope she enjoys the pregnancy part.'

'And you?'

'Me?'

'Do you want a million kids?'

'Yeah! Can't wait. And I'm doing the world a service by adding more of my DNA to the population.'

'But you don't worry about being like your dad?'

'What? No way. I'm completely different. And Valentina wouldn't let me behave like him, anyway.'

In the pause that followed, Rory wished he was more easy-going, and that he had his friend's breezy confidence.

'You think you're going to turn out like your dad?' Charlie asked.

Rory nodded.

'I'm presuming from the silence that you're nodding your head?'

He shrugged.

'Right, I see we're devolving into a cave bear, so I'll speak in words of one syllable,' Charlie replied. 'Would wife be with you if you be like dad?' he grunted like he was a caveman struggling to talk for the first time.

Rory huffed.

'Mum and dad of wife. They like you too? Much friend of wife like you, yes?'

'Hmmm.'

'Good. Cos me speak truth. Me best friend. Me know every—lots. All in world we know. Me—'

'Okay, I get it.'

Charlie laughed. 'Thank fuck. Speaking Caveman is hard work.'

'Valentina is a saint to put up with you twenty-four-seven.'

'Well, I am a god, or at least the World's Sexiest Man. Look, you've never been like your dad and you're not going to turn into him the moment your baby appears. If anything, you'll probably go so far the other way, you'll call your kid "Osprey Glen-Rainbow" and allow them to do whatever the fuck they like because you're "respecting their autonomy and right to creative expression".'

Rory snorted.

'Mate, you've got this. If you can cope with Brad Bauer as a stepfather, then you can cope with any—'

'*Not* my stepfather.'

'His mates still showing up for Christmas?'

'Yeah... We've got a couple of weeks to turn the castle into the bloody Downton Abbey Christmas special and it's not going well.'

'Not enough haggis and kilts to go around?'

'Mistletoe shortage and we underestimated how long it would take to decorate the castle the way they want it.'

'Well, at least you've got the Christmas lights sorted. You didn't cock that one up at all.'

'Fuck off.'

'They're phallus-tastic, dickity-boo, your most impressive erection to date.'

Rory sighed.

'Everything now better in Rory-land?' Charlie asked. 'Has my crisis line worked?'

'Yeah, thanks.'

'Excellent. Now just focus on Zoe and don't worry about Christmas. It'll all work out fine.'

December tenth. Thirty-five weeks + two

> Duncan: There's only one cracker left in
> the box

Rory: On my way

ENTERING THE BACK DOOR OF THE CASTLE AT A RUN, RORY leapt up the stairs. This latest message from Duncan informed him that things were extremely suboptimal in his wife's world, and he could hear the anguish in her voice carrying down the corridor as he strode towards the estate office door. God only knew how she'd react when she saw what was in his jacket pocket.

'How are they meant to have chestnuts roasting on an open fire when the chestnuts are already cooked, peeled and vacu-packed?' Zoe yelled into the phone as Rory entered the room.

He nodded at Duncan, who beat a hasty retreat. On the floor were cardboard boxes filled with provisions they'd ordered for Brad's friends, who were arriving in just over a week.

'And I ordered *mince* pies, not minced beef pies,' she continued. There was a pause. 'No! Mince pies as in the dried fruity things. You've sent sodding Fray Bentos ones with actual mince in them. And a bog-standard fruit cake is not, I repeat, *not*, an acceptable substitute for Christmas cake!'

Rory took Zoe's hand and gave it a squeeze.

'You don't seem to understand how important this is,' she said, her voice wavering. 'How important Christmas is. It's going to be ruined.' Her chin started to wobble. 'I'll call you back.'

She hung up and sobbed into his chest. 'It's a complete disaster. I can't seem to get anything right.'

'It's not your fault. We can order pies and cakes from Margaret at the bakery.'

'We can't. They wanted ones that came wrapped in cellophane and had some poncey label on. Honestly, Rory, I can't please them.' She raised her head. 'What are you doing back?'

He took a deep breath. It would be better if she found out in private.

'It's not the end of the world, but—'

'Oh my god, what's happened?'

'Shhhh, it's okay.'

He pulled a folded poster from his jacket pocket. It was advertising the Christmas ceilidh, and he'd found it stapled to a telegraph pole.

'This one's on me, Zoe. I'm sorry. The printers well and truly cocked it up.'

She opened it out. 'A Christmas *Kayleigh*?!'

The location, date and time were all correct, but the poster appeared to be advertising a little girl's birthday party. The baubles they'd discussed looked like balloons, and the background was more bubble gum pink than Santa red.

'I'm sorry, Zoe, it's my fault. They didn't seem to know what a ceilidh was and I didn't spell it for them.'

'Do the tickets say the same thing?' she asked faintly.

He nodded. 'I went to the post office. They've just been delivered and they all say Christmas Kayleigh.'

Zoe sank her head. '*The Courier* is going to have a fucking field day with this one. They're going to blame me because I'm English.'

'I'll tell them it was me.'

She sighed. 'They won't care. I don't think there's any way we can spin this.'

Rory pulled out his phone and rang Clive, the owner of Kinloch's only pub, who was supplying the bar for the ceilidh. He put it on speaker so Zoe could listen in.

'Clive, it's Rory and Zoe here. When's your Kayleigh's birthday?'

'Next month. It's her 21st. Why?'

'Have you seen the posters for the ceilidh yet?'

'No.'

'The printer fucked up big time, and it looks like we're throwing a party for her.'

'You're joking?'

'No.'

Clive laughed. 'God, she'll either be mortified or think it's the best thing ever.'

'I want to try and turn this around,' Rory continued. 'Could you speak to Kayleigh and ask if she wants to invite her friends? We can give her fifty free tickets if she's happy to turn this into an early birthday party?'

'Will do. I'll speak to her now and ring you back.'

'Thanks, Clive.'

Rory ended the call.

'Thank you.' Zoe smiled. 'That's a brilliant idea.'

He shrugged. 'First time for everything.'

'Nonsense. You're amazing. It's me who's falling apart.'

He pulled her into his arms. 'You're eight months pregnant and haven't taken a proper day off in weeks. You're doing great.'

'Did you get the tree for the entrance hall?'

'Yeah, want to go and see it?'

❧

Oh god. Just no.

Zoe bit the inside of her cheek to stop the scream of frustration escaping. She couldn't piss all over her husband's handiwork. Rory may have chopped down a tree taller than any cottage in Kinloch, but in the entrance hall of the castle it looked embarrassingly small.

She'd already vastly underestimated the volume of decorations needed to turn the castle into a Hallmark Christmas special, and now they were also dealing with a national shortage of mistletoe and holly.

Brad's friends were expecting a winter wonderland, but instead were going to get one from Poundland. The worst thing was that Rory had decorated the tree with every bauble they had, and it still looked completely under-dressed.

He had a worried frown on his face. 'Is it okay? It's the first tree I've ever decorated.'

Don't cry, don't cry, don't cry.

She burst into tears.

'Zoe, love, what's wrong? Just tell me and I'll fix it.'

'It's too small and you've gone to so much effort and I'm a terrible person and I can't cope and I'm losing my mind,' she wailed.

He ran his hands into his hair. 'I'll sort it. I'll find a way.'

'There isn't a way, Rory. We've run out of time, and I'm the one to blame. I wanted the extra ceilidh, the festival of lights, and the sodding Santa experience. I was the one who said yes to Brad's friends. Christmas is ruined, and it's all my fault!'

$\ast$ 8 $\ast$

December eighteenth. Thirty-six weeks + three

Zoe gazed at her reflection in the mirror and tried not to cry. *Again*.

It was the day Santa was visiting Kinloch Castle, and she was in a room just off the entrance hall, trying to fit her heavily pregnant body into an elf costume.

This had seemed a brilliant idea eight months ago, but even an extra-large costume wasn't going to cut it. The striped tights only made it as far as her mid-thigh, and the top was stuck above her bump.

She looked like an overstuffed sausage and felt like a beached whale.

This was her favourite time of the year, and she was finally going to be a mum. She should have been full of happiness. However, right now, she hated being pregnant and hated Christmas. Her stomach seemed unnaturally big, her ankles were swollen, she couldn't sleep, she needed to pee all the time, and her breasts had started leaking.

She felt guilty and ungrateful, and desperately missed her parents and her best friend, Sam. Her mum and dad had planned to stay home for Christmas, then travel up after Zoe gave birth in January and stay a month. But even if they changed their plans, there was nowhere for them to stay. Brad's friends were due in a couple of days and had hired the entire castle.

This Christmas was meant to be quiet, just her and Rory together in the cabin, but was now looking like more relentless work when she could barely even stay on her feet.

Taking off the elf costume, Zoe put her maternity trousers back on. They were down an elf, but at least Rory was still playing Father Christmas.

There was a knock at the door, then he entered, a big smile on his face.

'I bring glad tidings.'

Zoe looked at him askance. 'Have you been on the sherry?'

'Of great joy,' he continued.

Her jaw dropped. Rory looked relieved as well as happy. This was extremely strange.

'Who are you and what have you done with my husband?' she demanded.

Cradling her face, he brushed his lips across hers. 'I have done a good thing.'

'And that thing is?'

'Brad's friends aren't coming.'

She pulled back. 'What? They cancelled? But we need the money! We've spent—'

'Shhhh, it's okay. We're not refunding them anything.'

'What? How?'

'I rang Brad. I told him about the stress we're under, the mistletoe shortage and how we didn't want his friends to be disappointed.'

'You rang *Brad?*'

He nodded.

'He Who Shall Not Be Named?'

Rory grinned. 'Yup. And he persuaded them to swap coming here for a free stay at his place in Aspen, followed by Saint Barts.'

'And we don't have to give them their money back?'

'Nope.'

Zoe sank into a chair. 'Holy shit. So we can have a quiet Christmas, just the two of us?'

'Yes, or if you want, we can invite your parents?'

She welled up. 'Thank you, Rory. This is such a relief. I can't believe it.'

'Now all we need to do is get today over with, then you can put your feet up. You, me, Bandit, Basil and your beautiful bump. I promise I'll make Christmas perfect for you.'

Zoe swallowed her emotion. 'Okay, let's get you dressed as Santa and put some talc in your beard to make it white.'

Rory took off his work trousers and pulled on the red velour bottoms.

Oh god.

Being six foot six, they only reached his knees. It looked like he was wearing lederhosen.

Neither of them said a word.

He put the top on. It was big enough around the middle, but the sleeves ended just below his elbows. Zoe had deliberately ordered an XXL Santa suit, but it looked like an extra-small one on Rory's giant frame.

Yet another Christmas clusterfuck.

The ring of Rory's phone filled the silence.

'It's Brad.' He took the call.

'Dude!' Brad was so loud it sounded like he was in the room with them. 'Where are you, man?'

'We're in the castle.'

'Where?'

'Um, in the small study off the entrance hall. Why?'

The door flew open and Brad bounded in. 'Surprise!'

Zoe gripped Rory's hand as they stared at him in shock.

Barbara now entered and looked Rory up and down. 'Oh dear. That really won't do. Think of the children. You'll terrify them.'

Rory managed to recover first. 'Mum,' he croaked. 'What are you doing here?'

'Isn't it obvious? We're putting family first. You made it clear how much the two of you were struggling, and Zoe needs to rest.'

'But what about *Fight Dragon Club*?' Zoe asked. 'Isn't that meant to be filming now?'

Brad clicked his fingers. 'Rescheduled. I didn't want to miss the birth of my grandson.'

'I'm not due till mid-January,' Zoe said, feeling light-headed.

'Jesus says it's his time.'

'Jesús, Bradley. How many times do we have to have this conversation?'

'Sorry, Countess.'

Barbara raised her eyes theatrically, then clicked her fingers at Rory. 'Give Bradley the costume. We can take it from here.'

ZOE STOOD BEHIND BRAD IN THE CASTLE LIBRARY, NEXT TO the huge open fire, a clipboard in her hands, and watched him distil Christmas into the spirit of pure commercialism.

It hadn't started well.

She'd put out a chair for the children to sit on, but the first boy, who was clearly a fan, stood to attention in front of Brad.

'I want an Xbox,' he said loudly.

His mother stood behind her son, shaking her head at Brad.

'A bike,' she stage-whispered. 'He wants a bike.'

'Ho, ho, ho,' overacted Brad. 'I think what you *really* want is a bike.'

The little boy shook his head so hard Zoe was worried it might fly off.

'No! I want an Xbox.' There was a pause. 'Please?'

Brad slapped his thigh. 'Well, with manners like that, how can I refuse? One Xbox coming your way!'

The boy fist-pumped. 'Yessssss!'

His mother looked miserable.

Zoe dashed forward. 'You can't promise that,' she whispered in Brad's ear. 'She can't afford it.'

'Just take her details, babe. Father Bradmas has got this.'

It went downhill from there.

Within half an hour of Brad posting a photo of himself dressed as Santa, queues formed out of the castle for the chance to sit on his knee. And when word got out that he would provide whatever you asked for, the demands escalated.

'Are you *sure* you want a Tesla?' Brad asked a little girl who really should have been asking for two front teeth.

'Yeth,' she replied. 'A Tethla. And it hath to be...' she broke off to glance at her father.

'Deep blue metallic,' he said out of the corner of his mouth.

'Theep boo methallic,' she repeated.

NINETY MINUTES IN, RORY SHUT THE MAIN DOORS.

Ninety-one minutes in, fights broke out and people started smashing windows.

Shortly after, riot police arrived, along with two ambulances and the local press.

Barbara, toting a loaded shotgun, escorted Zoe out the back door and took her back to the cabin, then returned to the castle.

Zoe got into bed, cuddling Basil.

Merry Fucking Christmas.

December twenty-first. Thirty-six weeks+ six

IT WAS OFFICIAL. ZOE WAS DONE WITH BEING PREGNANT AND done with Christmas. She'd spent so long making the holiday magical for other people that there was no magic left for her. She was heavy and depressed, and nothing could lift her mood.

Rory was busy working outside, but she didn't even have the energy to ask about his days. She just stayed at the cabin with Bandit and Basil, hiding from everyone and counting the hours until her parents arrived.

That morning she'd woken with a dodgy stomach, and by the time Rory arrived back, late afternoon, she was ready for bed.

'Get dressed,' he said. 'We're going into town.'

'Don't want to,' she grumbled. 'I'm fed up and my tummy's upset. That steak we ate last night didn't agree with me.'

He frowned. 'I ate most of it and I'm okay. You think it's anything to do with the baby?'

She shrugged. 'Who knows? Pregnancy sucks and I could have another six weeks of it.'

'Well, there's a special carol service in Kinloch this evening and I really want to go.'

'Carols? *You?*'

'I think your love of Christmas has rubbed off on me.'

'I'm not in love anymore. It's all a load of consumerist bollocks. You were right. It's just another made-up holiday to be endured.'

Rory ran a hand through his hair. 'Zoe, I'm sorry I couldn't do more to take the strain off you. But I do want you to remember why you love Christmas.'

'And a carol concert will do that?'

'You never know. There's going to be candles. And mince pies.'

She rolled her eyes.

'Please? For me?'

She threw up her arms. 'Okay, okay. I'll do it. Can I get away with putting a coat over my pyjamas?'

He hesitated. 'If you don't mind the village seeing them?'

'I don't care right now. I've been trying for perfection, but everything's gone tits up no matter what I do.'

Throwing on her coat, hat and boots, Zoe followed Rory out to his truck, Bandit following. He'd been especially attentive recently and now wouldn't leave her side.

Rory drove them into Kinloch, parked in the back courtyard of the castle, and led her through the building into the great hall. It was already full of people, and everyone was holding a candle. With the main lights turned low, Zoe had to admit it was a beautiful sight.

Rory led her to the front, where one of the castle's wooden thrones had been placed.

'Are you sure I can sit?' she whispered. 'Everyone else is standing.'

'It's your castle, and no one else is eight and a half months pregnant,' he whispered back.

Zoe sank gratefully into the chair as the Kinloch community choir filed onto the raised dais at one end of the hall and began to sing.

'The angel Gabriel from heaven came,
his wings as drifted snow, his eyes as flame;
"All hail," said he, "thou lowly maiden Mary,
most highly favoured lady." Gloria.'

Zoe held her breath as the music filled the space. In the half-light, she could imagine this scene taking place hundreds, if not thousands, of years ago.

The carol ended, and Brad's voice rang out. 'And in the sixth month, the angel Gabrielle was sent from God into a city of Galilee called Nazareth.'

The choir parted, and a figure stepped forward, dressed all in white, with fairy wings and a tinsel halo.

Zoe's mouth fell open. *Sam?* But wasn't she meant to be working abroad?

Sam raised a magic wand in Zoe's direction and a spotlight suddenly shone on her chair.

Huh?

'Hail Mary, full of grace,' Sam declaimed. 'The Lord is with thee! Blessed art thou amongst women.'

Zoe turned to look at Rory, but he'd disappeared.

'Fear not, Mary,' Sam continued. 'For your husband shall returneth sooneth. He might have just poppeth out for a quick bathroom breaketh.' Laughter rippled around the room. 'Behold! Thou shalt conceive in thy womb, and bring forth a son or daughter, and thou shalt name him or her whatever the hell you chooseth.'

'Babe! Stick to the script!' Brad hissed from the side.

'The child shall be great, and the Lord God shall give unto him or her the throne of Rory his father; and he or she shall reign in the house of Kinloch forever.'

The audience applauded loudly.

'And Mary said unto the angel,' said Brad, looking pointedly at Zoe.

'Er,' Zoe began, trying to rack her brains for the next line. 'Um, but how has this happeneth? For I know not a man.'

'The Holy Ghost shall come upon thee,' said Sam. 'But in a totally consensual, non-creepy manner, so don't freaketh out.'

'And Mary said,' Brad continued.

Shit! What *did* Mary say? 'Um, thanks for that,' Zoe replied. 'Now you're here. Anything else I should know?'

'Not at all,' replied Brad quickly. 'Then the angel departed from her.' He gestured for Sam to move, but she didn't budge. 'Forthwith, and at great speed!' he continued.

'But the angel Gabrielle had just remembered a few more things to sayeth,' Sam said. 'Like how Mary is a hot milf, and she can totes see her and Gabrielle becoming BFF-eths.'

Brad stepped onto the dais in front of Sam, his hands raised to stop the laughter.

'And lo! There appeareth Joseph, who was most pleased because the Holy Ghost had come to him in a dream and explained the situation, so he was totally cool about everything.'

Rory returned to Zoe's side wearing a long jacket over his clothes that appeared to be made of sacking, and a tea towel on his head.

'What's going on?' she whispered to him.

'You only got to play the giraffe in your school's nativity, so I thought you deserved a crack at the main role.'

Taking another tea towel, he placed it on her head and secured it with a woven circlet.

Zoe's heart was so full she didn't know whether to laugh or cry.

'So, what happens next?' she asked.

'And it came to pass that a decree went out from Caesar Augustus that all the world should be registered,' said Brad.

'Joseph went up from Galilee to Bethlehem, to be registered with Mary, his betrothed wife, who was heavy with child.'

Rory held out his hand, and Zoe stood. The choir started singing 'Little Donkey' as they processed out of the hall, everyone following.

'Am I going to have to get on the back of a donkey?' she hissed.

He grinned. 'Just wait and see.'

❄ *9* ❄

Zoe exited the castle through the main entrance and started laughing. In front of her was an old open-topped carriage, and pulling it were two Highland cows. A sign was stuck to the side of the carriage with an arrow pointing at the cows and the word: 'DONKEY'.

One of the cows mooed loudly.

'Is that Zoe?' she asked excitedly.

Rory nodded. 'She was desperate to play the front half of the donkey.'

There was a loud noise as the other cow dumped a large pat on the cobbles.

'And that one's playing the back end,' he continued with a grin.

Rory helped her into the carriage and Bandit jumped in after.

'You're not sitting here with me?'

He shook his head. 'I'm going to lead them. And anyway, I wasn't sure how much weight they could pull.'

Brad had commandeered himself a megaphone and continued the story.

'And so, Mary and Joseph began their journey to Bethlehem!' he yelled. 'Picture the scene. Travelling alone through the desert: one pregnant virgin, one humble carpenter, and one donkey. The fate of the world resting in Mary's untouched womb.'

The cows set off at a slow pace through the courtyard, followed by the rest of the village with their candles. The choir was up ahead, on their umpteenth rendition of 'Little Donkey'.

A sharp pain suddenly sliced across Zoe's stomach and she gasped, clutching the side of the carriage.

It got stronger, stopping her breath as it tightened around her stomach.

Just as she thought she might pass out, it stopped.

What the ever-loving fuck was that?

There was no way this was labour. She wasn't due for another three weeks and knew most first-time mums gave birth ten days after their estimated date of delivery. Could it be Braxton Hicks contractions? She glanced around. People were smiling and chatting. Rory's attention was ahead with the cows. No one was looking at her.

Okay, breathe. Nothing to worry about. Chill the fuck out.

Another contraction slammed into her, squeezing her body till there was nothing left but blinding pain. This time, she remembered to breathe. Closing her eyes, she forced the air in and out. When it finally stopped, she was trembling.

Bandit whined and nudged up against her.

'It's okay, buddy. I'm fine.'

Zoe clenched her jaw to fight back tears. If this was indeed early labour, she wasn't going to survive. Wasn't it meant to be like period pain? Pop a couple of paracetamol, have a hot bath and go to bed? If she'd just had two mild contractions, then fuck only knew what major ones felt like. And she couldn't stop the nativity for a false alarm.

The procession paused at the bottom of the high street by a small area of grass where the war memorial stood. On it, behind a barrier, were three men trying to control a small flock of badly behaved sheep. Zoe saw Duncan, Fiona's younger brother, Jamie, and—

She blinked.

'Dad?'

Her father looked up and gave a wave. 'Hi, love!'

The sheep nearest him grabbed a mouthful of his robe and pulled. There was a loud rip and suddenly Arnold was showing the village his boxer shorts and knobbly knees.

'Behold,' yelled Duncan over the baaing of the sheep. 'I am sore afraid!'

'Aye,' continued Jamie. 'Me too. Is that an angel?'

'Sure is, babe,' replied Sam, giving him a wink.

'I bring you good news of great joy,' Brad shouted into his megaphone.

'Oi!' Sam yelled back. 'That's *my* line! For there is born to you this day—'

Zoe was hit by another wall of pain. She clutched Bandit's fur and tried to breathe through it.

'Fuck, fuck, fuck, fuck,' she muttered.

'A saviour who is Christ the lord or lady, and you will find him or her wrapped in bandages like a freaking mummy or something—'

'In a manger!' Brad screamed.

'I was just getting to that bit!'

The choir started singing 'While Shepherds Watched Their Flocks', as the sheep alternated between baaing and emptying their bowels. The noise was loud enough to drown out Zoe's frantic swearing.

Rory pulled the cows past the shepherds as her dad called out to her, 'See you in a bit, love!'

Zoe managed to wave before being hit with another freight train of a contraction. What had Fiona told her? Labour usually went on for days and wasn't serious unless she couldn't talk? At the moment she could still formulate a sentence, however, every word in it appeared to be 'fuck'.

As the pain passed, she caught her breath.

Rory turned. 'You enjoying yourself?' he asked with a smile.

Zoe gave him two thumbs up and managed a manic grin. He looked so happy. She wasn't going to ruin his surprise by making a fuss about nothing.

The choir continued singing as they proceeded down the high street towards the post office. Outside, dressed as if they'd been attacked by velour curtains from the nineteen seventies, stood Zoe's mum, as well as Fiona, and Fiona's mum, Morag. The choir segued into 'We Three Kings'.

When the carol finished, Morag spoke. 'We are three wise women who have been following a star.'

Brad leapt in front of them, wearing glow bands around his neck, head and wrists, and looking like an over-medicated raver who'd crashed into a school disco.

'That's me, baby! I'm the star!'

The crowd whooped and clapped, their attention thankfully away from Zoe as she braced against the side of the carriage, moaning in pain.

'We bring gifts of gold,' said Zoe's mum.

'Frankenstein,' added Morag.

'And Prosecco and spiced shortbread!' finished Fiona.

Everyone cheered.

As another contraction smacked into her, Zoe caught Sam's eye.

Her friend frowned and mouthed, *you okay?*

Zoe nodded, her nails digging into her thighs. It was all getting too much. She'd never experienced pain like this before. It was so intense and all-consuming she wanted to throw up. She needed to get through this nativity, then drive to Raigmore hospital. Right now, she didn't care if she was days or even weeks away from giving birth. She needed pain relief right now. That, or sudden death.

She ran the nativity story through her head. Hopefully, they would skip Herod and the massacre of the innocents. What was still left? Brad was now telling everyone how Mary and Joseph had survived the journey to Bethlehem and were trying to find somewhere to stay.

The procession stopped outside The King's Arms, and Rory knocked on the door.

Clive opened it.

'Kind sir,' Rory started. 'My wife is heavy with child and we need a place to stay.'

'There's no room at the inn,' said Clive.

A contraction slammed into Zoe and she screamed with pain.

'See?' declaimed Rory, dramatically. 'The baby draws near!'

'Sorry, mate. No can do,' Clive replied, crossing his arms in front of his chest.

The crowd booed and Bandit barked.

Zoe was now panting to stay conscious.

'Not even a lowly stable?' Rory asked.

Clive sighed theatrically. 'Well, I suppose you could use it as long as you stay out of the way of the oxen. It's back down yonder high street in the community centre.'

'Thank you,' Rory replied. 'We shall travel there forthwith.'

He turned the cows in a slow circle and they started back down the road.

Zoe closed her eyes. She couldn't take anything else in. She was vaguely aware of singing and laughing, and Bandit licking her hand, but most of her concentration was taken up in preparing for the battering waves of agony that relentlessly assaulted her. She was lost in a turbulent sea of pain that crashed through without mercy.

'Behold!' yelled Brad into his megaphone.

Zoe opened her eyes. In front of them, at the end of a small car park, was the entrance to the community centre. A large sign above the door read 'LOWLY STABLE', and a beautifully decorated Christmas tree stood to the side. The crowds fell silent as the choir sang 'Oh Tannenbaum'.

Another contraction slammed into her, and she screamed.

'Zoe?' Rory dropped the halter holding the cows and rushed to the side of the carriage. 'What's wrong?'

She panted, unable to get any words out, her eyes scrunched closed.

The carriage lurched forwards.

Bandit barked loudly.

Zoe opened her eyes to see the cows heading straight for the tree.

Rory leapt up next to her. 'What's happening? Is it the baby?'

There was a crash, and the carriage stopped with a jolt. The cows had knocked the tree over and were investigating the decorations.

'Let's get you inside,' Rory said, then lifted her out of the carriage and carried her into the building.

Zoe could hear Bandit snarling and growling at the door, preventing anyone from following them.

The community centre was small and had only one main room, which had been decorated to look like a stable, with loose straw and bales on the floor.

Rory placed her gently onto a bale and she fell forward

onto her hands and knees, circling her hips and lowing like a cow.

'Is this labour?'

She nodded, her whole body undulating with pain.

'Fuck! Hang on. I'll go get help.'

Her hand shot out to grip his wrist. 'Don't. Leave. Me,' she panted.

'But—'

She dug her nails into his arm.

'Okay. I won't leave. I promise. What can I do?'

'Need. Pyjamas. Off,' she managed.

'Someone call an ambulance!' Rory shouted. 'I think she's having the baby!'

Zoe clung to him as he held her up and tugged off her pyjama bottoms. Her body had been completely taken over by labour, and all she could do was hang on for dear life as the pain moved down in waves.

In the background, she could just about make out people yelling her name and Bandit barking and growling.

Suddenly she had an overwhelming urge to push. 'It's coming!'

Rory pulled off her coat. 'I've got you, Zoe. I'm here.'

She was on her knees, facing him. Rory held under her shoulders, kissing the side of her head and reassuring her.

'I love you. You've got this. It's okay.'

A stinging circle of pain stretched her as another massive contraction bore down. There was no going back. This was happening and there was nothing she could do to stop it.

'Rory!' she screamed as she felt her baby's head pop out. There was a lull, and she caught her breath.

She stared into Rory's worried eyes. 'The head's out,' she panted. 'You need to be ready to catch them.'

His face was pale, but he nodded. 'Just let me know when.'

Another contraction rolled through. 'Now!'

Zoe held around Rory's neck as his hands moved between her legs.

The baby slipped out.

'I've got them,' he said. 'I've got them.'

She fumbled to open her top and Rory lifted the baby to rest on her chest, cradling the two of them in his massive arms. They looked down at their child. It had a shock of ginger hair and deep dark eyes that stared up at them solemnly.

'Oh my god,' Zoe gasped, her body filled with a rush of overwhelming love. 'We did it.'

They held each other, their baby between them, as they cried and laughed.

'You're incredible,' Rory whispered.

'Me or the baby?'

'You, hands down. But this little one is pretty incredible too.'

'What's going on in there?' Barbara yelled from the front door. 'Bandit won't let anyone in!'

The baby let out a loud cry.

'It's a boy!' screamed Brad.

Rory shook his head as the choir launched into 'Joy to the World'.

Zoe angled the baby towards her breast and it immediately latched on.

'Shall we see what we've got?' she asked.

Rory nodded and carefully moved the umbilical cord to one side. 'I think it's a girl,' he said, sounding dazed.

'Are you sure?'

He lifted one leg up. 'Yes. I can confirm there is no penis to be found.'

Zoe kissed her daughter's head. 'Thank you for proving everyone wrong,' she whispered.

EPILOGUE

Christmas Day

Rory padded quietly around the inside of the cabin, Shona cradled against his bare chest. Even though his daughter seemed to have a talent for sleeping that rivalled her mother's, he couldn't help the one-sided conversation that flowed from him like a river into the loch.

'So, even though your mummy is currently sparko, when she wakes up, it's very important to have a cup of tea ready. Especially now she's also responsible for feeding you, little one,' he whispered. 'Although the kettle boiling might be too noisy. Maybe we should go for a walk with Bandit?'

Shona stirred, her tiny lips smacking together. Rory's heart was suddenly too big for his chest, love overflowing from it and flooding his insides.

He kissed her forehead. 'I love you, Shona.'

A groan came from the bed as Zoe opened her eyes. 'What time is it?' she mumbled.

'Nearly half ten. We're due at the castle at twelve. Happy Christmas.'

'We can't have sex for the next six weeks.'

'Er... I wasn't trying to?'

'Well, the sight of you shirtless and holding a baby is inspiring me to make more, so try and make yourself a little less attractive.'

He smiled. 'I haven't brushed my hair.'

'You never brush it.'

Rory sat on the edge of the bed and handed Shona to Zoe for the morning feed.

'I can't believe she's here,' she said quietly. 'We're so lucky.'

Rory squeezed her hand. He'd never been one for displays of emotion, but he seemed to be on an oxytocin high that was never going down.

'It's snowing,' he said.

'Will we be able to get to the castle?'

'Yes, it's only light, but it looks really pretty. You'll love it.'

Zoe smiled. 'This is the best Christmas ever.'

'So far. Don't forget we've got to survive lunch.'

'Do you know who's in charge?'

Rory raised an eyebrow. 'Who do you think? Mum and Brad are incapable of relinquishing control of anything to anyone. Thank god your folks are so easy-going.'

'There'll be others to help, too.'

'Yes, it should be fun.'

Zoe stared at him as if he'd just grown another head. 'Fun? You're looking forward to Christmas Day?'

He grinned. 'Your obsession has rubbed off on me. I'm a changed man.'

She ran her fingers down his jaw. 'Well, the beard has gone at any rate.'

'Do you miss it?'

'I prefer you like this. I can see more of your gorgeous face.'

'Maybe I can grow it for next year. And find a Santa costume that actually fits.'

'Ooh yes! And I'll dress up as Mrs Claus and Shona can be an elf. We can do it in November. It can be our Christmas card.'

Rory shook his head, but couldn't stop the laugh from escaping. 'I see you've rediscovered your love of Christmas.'

'Yes, I think I have. But now it's even more exciting because we can make it special for Shona.'

THAT AFTERNOON, SITTING AROUND THE TABLE IN THE dining room, Rory knew he'd made his peace with Christmas, *and* being a father. He was wearing a paper hat and sharing cracker jokes with Brad, as everyone else laughed at the terrible jokes. His mother's sharp edges had been smoothed by copious amounts of Morag's sloe gin, and Barbara appeared besotted with her granddaughter.

Shona didn't seem fazed by the noise or being passed around for cuddles, and Zoe couldn't stop smiling. Rory felt her happiness filling every part of him. They were full of good food and surrounded by their family and friends. Even Charlie had joined them for a chat from Colombia with the whole of Valentina's family yelling in the background and demanding to see the baby.

After lunch, they relaxed in the library in front of a roaring fire. Brad wheeled in a massive TV, and they all watched *A Muppet Christmas Carol*, which had just nudged ahead of *Die Hard* in a vote they'd had earlier for the best Christmas film, and afterwards, Jamie got out his guitar and he and Sam took requests.

Rory let the music wash over him, with Zoe and Shona cradled in his arms. The run up to Christmas had been the most stressful time of his life, but right now it all seemed like a distant memory. Now, with his wife and baby daughter, and surrounded by love, everything was right with Rory's world. Everything was perfect.

THE END

❧

Thank you so much for reading Christmas Games!

Next up, read **Love ad Lib**, the hilarious fake-dating romcom set in Somerset with buttoned-up Lord Henry Foxbrooke and free-spirited actress Libby Fletcher!

Evie's books are available worldwide in all formats from:
www.eviealexanderbooks.com

REVIEW CHRISTMAS GAMES
WRITE A REVIEW & MAKE MY DAY!

Thank you so much for reading Christmas Games! I hope you enjoyed reading it as much as I enjoyed writing it!

Even if just a couple of lines (or a star rating), writing a review is the most amazing thing you can do! It helps people find my books, and lets them know what you loved about them.

You can review Christmas Games at:
Apple
Amazon
Bookbub
Goodreads
Kobo
Barnes & Noble
Google Play
And any other storefront or platform you use!

And, if you want to share more about Christmas Games on social media or your blog, please help yourself to our library of graphics, elements and more via the link below!

www.eviealexanderauthor.com/christmas-games/

Thank you!

Evie ♡

READ LOVE AD LIB

**After all the fun and games in the Scottish Highlands,
head to Somerset for the Foxbrooke series!**

LOVE AD LIB

Shy and reserved Lord Henry Foxbrooke needs a fake
girlfriend. Free-spirited actress Libby Fletcher needs a job. But
when they arrive in Somerset for Henry's birthday
celebrations, neither are prepared for their reception.

As friendship blurs and faking it starts to feel a little too real,
disaster strikes. Can Libby and Henry stick to the script, or
has their entire act just bombed?

Tropes

Small Town, Fake Dating, Grumpy/Sunshine, Opposites
Attract, One Bed, Different Worlds, Fish-out-of-Water

Available in print, Ebook and audiobook, get your copy

of Love ad Lib from Evie's Shopify store now by going to:

www.eviealexanderbooks.com

NEWSLETTER SIGN-UP

Newsletter freebies are waiting, just for you...

In my newsletter you get Evie news before anyone else, as well as exclusive content and goodies.

Newsletter subscribers are my extra special friends, and get everything from bonus epilogues, 19,000 words of deleted sex scenes, free stories, free audiobooks, extracts from my current work-in-progress, and exclusive offers and giveaways.

Sign up now!

www.eviealexanderauthor.com/subscribe

SEX INDEX
(AKA THE GOOD BITS)

There have been many great contributions to the world of literature. Gutenberg invented the printing press, Shakespeare invented romantic comedy, and J K Rowling invented Harry Potter. However, all of these achievements pale into insignificance compared to my contribution – the sex index.

Here you can easily find and re-read the most steamy scene from Christmas Games. Enjoy...

Page 62 – Breaking out Big Bob...

And if that wasn't enough, don't forget I've got nineteen thousand words of super-hot deleted sex scenes from Highland and Hollywood Games available exclusively for newsletter subscribers.

If you want some extra action, get yourself signed up today at:

www.eviealexanderauthor.com/subscribe

ACKNOWLEDGMENTS

Christmas Games is dedicated to my daughter, Elway. My gloriously funny, miracle IVF baby. You are the best luck I've ever had and I love to the ends of the universe and back. Thank you for everything you bring to my life xxx

Thank you to this book's editing team of Aimee Walker, Mike Thomas, Margaret Amatt, and Mike AF. Thank you to Bailey McGinn for designing another wonderful cover and Mark Karasick for taking such fabulous photos of me.

Thank you to my outstandingly supportive friends, in particular my alpha reader, Pash, who has been my biggest cheerleader right from before the very beginning, and Margaret (again), who indulges me on a daily basis.

My team at Emlin Press: Victoria, Mandy, and Liezl. Thank you for doing everything I can't, won't, or don't have time for. Thank you for tolerating my foul mouth, laughing at my unfunny jokes and sticking around.

Thank you to my husband for his support and being the best father to our daughter I could ever have wished for.

And last, but by no means least, I want to thank my fabulous ARC team, the incredible online community of book lovers and YOU, the reader! Thank you for your continued support and for reading Rory and Zoe's crazy Christmas baby story. Each time you read my books, write me a review and recommend me in countless different ways, my heart gets a little fuller. Thank you!

Evie ♡

Ps - I love love LOVE hearing from my readers so please get in touch via email or social media to ask me anything or just tell me about your day!

ALSO BY EVIE ALEXANDER

Get all of Evie's books in print, audio, or eBook format, as well as special offers, early releases, and exclusive deals at www.eviealexanderbooks.com

THE KINLOCH SERIES

HIGHLAND GAMES

Zoe's given up everything for a ramshackle cabin in Scotland. She wants a new life, but her scorching hot neighbour wants her out. As their worlds collide, will Rory succeed in destroying her dream? Or has he finally met his match? Let the games begin...

Tropes

Small Town, Enemies-to-Lovers, Grumpy/Sunshine, Fish-out-of-Water, Opposites Attract, Forced Proximity

HOLLYWOOD GAMES

In a last-ditch attempt to save Kinloch castle, new lovers Rory and Zoe throw open the doors to a Hollywood superstar. But when it all goes south, it's up to them to rewrite the script, save the castle's future, and find their own happy ending.

Tropes

Small Town, Soulmates, Grumpy/Sunshine, Fish-out-of-Water

KISSING GAMES

Bodyguard Charlie has a new mission: teach workaholic Hollywood actress Valentina how to play, one wild adventure at a time. But when no-strings fun turns into something more, they have to face some hard truths. Can they find a future together, or will their love remain a Highland fling?

Tropes

Small Town, Dark Secrets, Bodyguard/Actress, Forced Proximity, Alpha-roll hero, Dating Game

MUSICAL GAMES

After lying to a Hollywood megastar, Sam needs Jamie to write an album with her in just ten days He's got the voice of an angel and the body of a god, but fame is the last thing on his mind. Will he help make her dreams come true?

Tropes

Small Town, Grumpy/Sunshine, Male Virgin, Cinnamon Roll Hero, Opposites Attract, Fish-out-of-Water, Forced Proximity

WEDDING GAMES

Rory and Zoe want to get married. Not easy when their mothers are mortal enemies and Rory's step-father is a Hollywood star with a death wish. Can they unravel the tangles in time to tie the knot, or is eloping the only answer? Get ready for Scotland's wedding of the year!

Tropes

Small Town, Grumpy/Sunshine, Opposites Attract, Soulmates, Fish-out-of-Water

CHRISTMAS GAMES

Having a baby's easy, right? Until wayward in-laws, an out-of-control cow and mad Santa get in the way. All Rory and Zoe want is a relaxing Christmas before their baby arrives, but straightforward is not their style...

Tropes

Small Town, Grumpy/Sunshine, Opposites Attract, Soulmates, Fish-

THE FOXBROOKE SERIES

ONE NIGHT IN FOXBROOKE

When chef Ben 'Kenobi' Walker gets the call to help save a VIP dinner at Foxbrooke Manor, he doesn't expect to run into old flame Leia Perry. She's all grown up and even more attractive than when they were teenagers – but she hasn't forgotten what happened ten years ago, and she *definitely* hasn't forgiven him. Will one night give Ben the second chance he needs to prove himself and win back Leia's heart?

Tropes

Small Town, Second Chance, Return to Hometown, Enemies-to-Lovers, Bet, Brother's Best Friend, Work Colleagues, Forced Proximity, First Love, Reverse Grumpy-Sunshine, Opposites Attract

LOVE AD LIB

Shy and reserved Lord Henry Foxbrooke needs a fake girlfriend. Free-spirited actress Libby Fletcher needs a job. But when they arrive in Somerset for Henry's birthday celebrations, neither are prepared for their reception. As friendship blurs and faking it starts to feel a little too real, disaster strikes. Can Libby and Henry stick to the script, or has their entire act just bombed?

Tropes

Small Town, Fake Dating, Grumpy/Sunshine, Opposites Attract, One Bed, Different Worlds, Fish-out-of-Water

AN UNHOLY AFFAIR

Gorgeous Jack Newton has fallen in love with Eveline Shaw. But she's a female vicar dreaming of marriage and kids, and he's a male escort heading out of town. Can Jack show Eveline heaven and keep his secret safe, or are they both headed straight for hell?

Tropes

Small Town, Forbidden Love, Love at First Sight, Sworn off a Relationship, Priest, Different Worlds, Opposites Attract, Dark Secret

THE UPPER CRUSH

James Hunter-Savage is a cocky city boy who isn't used to anyone else taking the reins. Lady Estelle Foxbrooke is a fiery country girl who's about to show him who's boss. Can they learn to fight for love rather than with each other, or will their love hate relationship destroy everything they're working for?

Tropes

Small Town, Enemies-to-Lovers, Alpha Hero, Love/Hate, Playboy in Love, Different Worlds, Workplace Romance, Fake Dating

THE LOVE POSITION

Beautiful academic, Sophia Hunter-Savage, has run away to an ashram to reinvent herself. Hot yoga teacher, Isaac Hayward, has left town to avoid the only woman able to tempt him off the spiritual path.

But karma sucks.

Now Isaac's teaching Sophia and they're finding themselves in all kinds of unexpected positions. Will their forbidden love bring inner peace and happiness, or end in a tangled mess?

Tropes

Forbidden Love, Opposites Attract, Teacher/Student, Sworn off a Relationship, Forced Proximity, Love at First Sight, Different Worlds, Fish-out-of-Water

CHRISTMAS OFF SCRIPT

Best friends, Leo Foxbrooke and Ella Chamberlain, have never been single at the same time. Until now... Playing Cinderella and Prince Charming in the Christmas pantomime, their on-stage chemistry kindles an unexpected spark behind the scenes. Can they rewrite their friendship this festive season and finally unwrap true love?

Tropes

Small Town, Friends-to-Lovers, Best Friend's Ex, Oblivious to Love, Unrequited Love, Fake Relationship

ONE NIGHT ONLY

Pop star Avery Taylor craves a break from her public life, and a one-night stand with a stranger feels like the perfect escape. A year later, while recovering from an injury, she's stunned to find her nurse is Connor Foxbrooke, the man who touched her soul that night. Avery is ready to break the rules for love, but Connor, who values his quiet life, fears heartbreak. With Avery set to return to the spotlight as soon as she's recovered, can they bridge their worlds and turn their one night into forever?

Tropes

Second-Chance, Mistaken Identity, One Night Stand, Different Worlds, Opposites Attract, Injury, Forced Proximity, Fish-out-of-Water, Celebrity, Pop Star, Small Town

RIGHTING MR WRONG

Mooning a party of nuns is bad for anyone, but for TV star Aiden Wilder, it's catastrophic. Enter Willow Foxbrooke, a quiet PR worker who's tasked with saving his reputation through a fake relationship. As Willow teaches him how to recover his image, they start to fall for each other. But how can true love grow from something that was never real to begin with?

Tropes

Small Town, Fake Dating, Grumpy/Sunshine, Celebrity, Opposites Attract, Different Worlds, Fish-out-of-Water

UNDER THE INFLUENCER

Sunny Summer Foxbrooke's career as an Influencer is over. Now she's forced to work with grumpy Finn Oakley, the man who's avoided her for years. Will Finn finally return her love, or will she always just be his best friend's little sister?

Tropes

Brother's best friend, Grumpy/Sunshine, Beauty and the Beast, Age Gap, Unrequited Love, Rivals, Different Worlds, All Grown Up, Small Town

※

By Evie Alexander and Kelly Kay

EVIE & KELLY'S HOLIDAY DISASTERS SERIES

Evie and Kelly's Holiday Disasters are a series of hot and hilarious romantic comedies with interconnected characters, focusing on one holiday and one trope at a time.

CUPID CALAMITY

Featuring **Animal Attraction** & **Stupid Cupid**

Patrick and Sabina have ditched their blind dates for each other. Ben's fighting a crazed chimp for Laurie's love. Insta-love meets insta-disaster in these laugh-out-loud Valentine's day novellas.

COOKOUT CARNAGE

Featuring **Off With a Bang** & **Up in Smoke**

Cute farm boy Jonathan clings to a love ideal, blissfully ignoring what the universe has planned, while keeping track of his pet pig. Posh Brit follows his heart into the American Midwest in search of Sherilyn, his digital dream love.

CHRISTMAS CHAOS

Featuring **No way in a Manger** & **No Crib and No Bed**

In Scotland, Zoe and Rory attempt to have a civilised and respectable rite of passage, but straightforward is not their style. In Sonoma, Bax and Tabi attempt to throw a meaningful Christmas celebration. But there are too many people involved and it's nothing like they expect.

Get Evie's books in all formats as well as special offers, early releases, and exclusive deals direct from her website:

www.eviealexanderbooks.com

ABOUT THE AUTHOR

Evie Alexander is a multi-award-winning author of sexy romantic comedies, blending snort-laugh humour and panty-melting chemistry into unputdownable stories that will steal your heart.

When she's not dreaming up swoony heroes and relatable heroines, Evie can be found in the beautiful West Country of the UK, where she lives with her ridiculously patient husband, miracle daughter, and two dogs who think they run the show.

eviealexanderbooks.com

www.eviealexanderauthor.com

instagram.com/eviealexanderauthor
facebook.com/eviealexanderauthor
x.com/Evie_author
bookbub.com/authors/evie-alexander
amazon.com/Evie-Alexander/e/B08ZJGLP29?ref=sr_ntt_s-rch_lnk_1&qid=1630667484&sr=8-1
pinterest.com/eviealexanderauthor